DB855916

THE SOCIETY
BALL MURDERS

THE SOCIETY BALL MURDERS

Jack Albin Anderson

Walker and Company
New York

First published in the United States of America in 1990
by Walker Publishing Company, Inc.
Published simultaneously in Canada by Thomas Allen & Son
Canada, Limited, Markham, Ontario
Library of Congress Cataloging-in-Publication Data
Anderson, Jack Albin
The society ball murders / Jack Albin Anderson
ISBN 0-8027-5766-9
I. Title.
PS3551.N367S6   1990
813'.52—dc20   90-12062
CIP

Printed in the United States of America
2 4 6 8 10 9 7 5 3 1

To
Ash Green
and
my wife Gail

"What is not good for the hive is not good for the bee."
—Marcus Aurelius at a wine and cheese tasting.
131 A.D.

THE SOCIETY
BALL MURDERS

▽

My Job

THE HUMAN APPENDIX IS described in medical texts as "a vestigial organ of no use to human beings; it is only important when it becomes inflamed and infected, when immediate surgery is then necessary in order to remove the appendage."

That describes my old job, society writer for the *San Francisco Journal*, biggest and best read paper in Northern California.

Though research always showed PATTIES CHATTER the least read segment of the paper, it continued to run seven days a week, oiling the egos of San Francisco's rich social set. The Huntting-Margate's, wealthy owners of the *Journal*, leading socialites and fourth generation San Franciscans (their ancestors made it through Donner Pass, the Mayflower of the West), would hardly allow their newspaper to ignore the city's aristocracy.

With boring regularity my column featured the same old designer gowned benevolents who staged benefits for every cause and incurable disease in sight. Charity balls, luncheons, wine tastings, cheese sampling, boat rides, show openings, fashion shows and balloon ascensions . . . absolutely no end to the stupid things. One "do" I covered, for instance, was a picnic staged by "Friends of the San Fran-

1

cisco Zoo" to launch the new Quackenbush Monkey Pavillion, and right in the middle of Mayor Marge Bronsterns'
ribbon cutting speech, a couple of horny, smiling orangutans
began to stroke themselves wildly while staring at little
Binky Crenshaw in her flaming red Adolfo strapless.

Fearing old Mrs. Huntting-Margate would have a connip-
tion and fire us both, my editor deleted my line about the
"passionate primates of the pavillion." I could never have
any fun with my column.

I suppose the ladies mean well with all their charity things
but they seem oblivious to the idea that their parties are
supposed to actually make a few bucks for the needy and
unfortunate. With all the benefit balls staged last year by our
city's ubiquitous matrons, Neenie Haverstock and Binky
Crenshaw, there wasn't enough money left to keep a Tenderloin wino in supermarket burgundy for a week. On the
other hand, the money Binky paid designers for her ball
gowns could have kept the Salvation Army in uniforms and
money pots for decades.

How did I become a society writer? . . . A girl from humble,
middle class beginnings? I was a journalism student at
Berkeley when I met Charlie Nottingham III—pronounced
Notting'mm—old San Francisco, Social Register, the works,
at the Big Game at Stanford in 1968. We fell in love and
married right after graduation. No children though. I think
Charlie's sperm count was a bit low, plus he was always a
little limp in that department anyway. But we had some good
times.

Charlie knew the Huntting-Margates socially and introduced me to old Mrs. Huntting-Margate who coerced one of
her editors into hiring me as an entry-level reporter—entry-
level meaning a notch above "john" attendant.

I wrote up announcements of ladies' club meetings, ad-
vancing rapidly to obituaries, and thanks to my blue-book
husband, began covering charity balls and parties run by old
and new money. In those early years I wasn't exactly ugly,

and Charlie dressed me well enough to blend with the ball followers. But after a few years of cocktails and cheese puffs, my cute little figure was no longer cute or little.

So there I was at the half-million circulation *Journal*, turning in social placenta for a column read avidly by a few hundred people who rushed to the paper every morning to see their names in boldface type sprinkled among sentences about the venison consomme and brandied quail eggs served at their last ball.

My Boss

 M Y EDITOR, PETER KNAPP, and I got along fairly well; he realized the inanity of the stuff I wrote and sympathized with me. But even so, he was always on my back to punch it up a little.

"Do those Binky and Dodie people do anything besides go to parties, for godsake? Certainly they must do something else you can write about."

"You'll be sorry," I said, "when I explode with gout from all the duck mousse I stuff myself with for your precious paper."

He smiled, reaching across his desk, squeezing my hand. "Sorry, Patty, but you know what I mean. The column's such a fucking bore. Your obituaries had more bite."

Peter never said fuck unless he was serious.

I stuck out my tongue at him—playfully though because he was my boss—and walked out of his office. I had to go home and get ready to cover a benefit for the Institute of International-something-or-other at the Fairmont Hotel, where tables of ten were going for only $5,000, including grey roast beef.

By then I was used to walking into my lonely apartment. Two years before when Charlie Notting'mm was running low in the money department, he'd left me for a rich old widow he'd met when we were covering the Organ Donors Ball. No, I won't say it. I hope Charlie's happy.

I went to my bedroom, and for the hundredth time slipped on my size 14 threadbare black ball dress, garnished with my fabulous Ciro's fake diamond collection I'd bought on sale, thinking how I could spice up my "such a fucking bore" column. It wasn't a gossip column. I wasn't allowed that luxury; my orders were to be discreet. Gossip for the *Journal* was written by young Bert Walker who's still there. Bert's a flaming liberal who makes a fortune, cries about the downtrodden, demeans the conservatives and goes everywhere at the drop of a jet with and on the richest Republicans in town.

I was the poor schlemiel who wrote about shallow socialites and cloying climbers, weaving their names through boring crap about museum luncheons, opera openings, and hilarious cocktail parties.

At one desperate moment I had an idea how to unbore my column: invent a couple of obscenely rich, crazy fictional characters who move into town and begin throwing wild, exotic, erotic events. I figured my readers would die to know who they were, but my journalistic integrity would preclude divulging such information. But I was chicken. Mrs. Huntting-Margate would have destroyed me if she'd found out.

Anyway, I was feeling useless and miserable writing such junk every day.

▽

The Stiff

THAT NIGHT I COVERED the dreary International Institute-for-Whatever dinner dance at the Fairmont Grand Ballroom; same old faces in designer gowns and black-tie milling around with their tinkling drinks, waiting for the lights to dim, ordering them to their dinner tables. "Hi Bucky, hi Binky, hi Dudley, hi Buffy, hi Dodie; Nice to see you; *So* nice to see you; Back from Pebble? Traveling again?; Love your gown *dahling*."

Westerners with mid-Atlantic accents.

Eddie, my faithful photographer, and I were shooting couples, checking their names and their gown designers. Queen of the climbers, Sophie Jacobs, came up to me with her garlic breath and caviar-studded teeth and started buttering me up like she always does. One more lift and her face would snap like a strained window shade . . . and she was flashing a thousand carats. Grotesque old thing. Her husband, Morris (in this town anyone can buy into society), made a fortune as city slumlord; owned all the rundown hotels in the Tenderloin. Now they were in the social swim, buying every inch of their way, backing old Broadway shows and putting wings on hospitals. And Morris (who could blame him) was screwing every chorus girl and nurse he could get his hands on.

After the last-drink-before-dinner panic, the little temporary bars closed and everyone carried their white wines, scotches and martinis to their tables, numbered 1 through 57. To keep euphoria alive, they began popping open the bottles of donated wine already at the tables.

Nobody heard the black speaker from the Institute-of-Whatever. The crowd was chattering, clanking glasses and silverware, ignoring the poor man droning on about his obscure organization. Through the rude noises, we heard an occasional guilt-provoking word or phrase—"doomed, hunger and despair, human rights, involvement, Third World conflict." Filthy rich Monty Delacorte, who in his spare time arranged tours for his rich friends, was probably thinking of doing one of the Third World in Vuitton-upholstered Land Rovers.

The spokesman finished and the dancing began. Chairwoman Binky Crenshaw had flown out at great expense Eddie Frecker's current hot stuff New York two/four society dance band who began playing chestnuts from *Le Cage aux Folles* and *My Fair Lady* at about 90 miles an hour. Frecker's schtick and claim to social fame was sweating and banging his piano unmercifully throughout the evening without ever stopping for a break. We figured Eddie sweat so much he didn't have to wee wee, but he let his sidemen sneak off one at a time.

Dot-dot-dottyah-dot-dot-dottyah—every other tune was "New York, New York." I'd heard it a thousand times at every ball I'd covered. But the crowd, half in the bag, loved it because it was about the only song they could remember.

By the end of the evening the waiters had stolen most of the de Larenta and Polo cologne samples from the tables and San Francisco's cream of the crop were lined up at the coat check to retrieve their sables, minks and lynx from the poor little immigrant boat people scurrying around behind the counter.

The ballroom cleanup crew swooped in to clear the tables,

getting ready for the next night's benefit for Alzheimer's Disease, which Dodie Wellingham had unwittingly named "A Night to Remember."

A few column-climbers had cornered me just outside the ballroom and suddenly we heard a hell of a commotion from the cleanup crew. I ran in to find out what was going on and I saw the crew, screaming in every language but English, staring at a skinny little woman still at her table. I walked closer; maybe some hot stuff for my "such a fucking bore" column, I thought.

Sitting straight up, stiff as a board, smiling and still clutching her fluted glass of bubbling champagne, was Binky Crenshaw. She looked like a figure in the Wax Museum at Fisherman's Wharf.

$\triangledown$

The Barbecue

*P*ATTIE'S CHATTER *OCT. 28, 1989 San Francisco Journal*

. . . AT LAST NIGHT'S GALA "INTERNATIONAL INSTITUTE FOR THE ADVANCEMENT OF THE LESSER WORLD" DINNER AT THE FAIRMONT GRAND BALLROOM, DECORATED IN AFRICAN SAFARI THEME AND BLESSED WITH THE TOE-TAPPING MUSIC OF NEW YORK'S EDDIE FRECKER, OUR OWN TIRELESS BINKY CRENSHAW, WEARING A STUNNING RED SEQUINED BALLENCIAGA ORIGINAL, DRANK HER LAST DOM PERIGNON TOAST. HUBBY DUDLEY CRENSHAW, OF THE CALIFORNIA MELON DYNASTY, MISSED HER LAST MOMENTS, HAVING GONE TO THE COAT CHECK TO GET BINKY'S OPERA-LENGTH RUSSIAN SABLE, DESIGNED BY MARGO . . . MORE ABOUT BINKY IN TOMORROW'S OBITS . . . MEANWHILE A WARM CIAO FROM ALL OF US BINKY DEAR . . .

THE HUNTLEY HAVERSTOCKS SPENT ANOTHER FUN-CRAMMED WEEKEND WITH EFFIE AND GRAMM HARKNESS AT PEBBLE—etc.

A reporter friend told me Dudley Crenshaw rode with Binky in the ambulance to St. Francis Hospital where the Crenshaw's family physician, Doctor Broderick, joined them shortly after. Broderick examined Binky and pronounced her dead of a massive stroke.

Next day at the luncheon benefit for Dogs for the Deaf (I still don't understand this one), the talk was all about Binky. What happened? Food poisoning? What caused the stroke? Too much Liposuction? Starvation at the Fat Farm?

Whatever it was, she was dead. Just like that. I know dead people stiffen from rigor mortis, but not as fast as she did. Her 105 pound, scrawny little diet-ridden body was still in the sitting position when the two Korean busboys carried her from the table. And though they'd pried loose the champagne glass, her tiny hand had remained in her favorite clutch/toast mode. A touching sight.

We knew Binky wasn't fifty yet. Damn near but not yet. But with the help of all her skin tucking and fat sucking, she looked in her late thirties, if you didn't get too close. She must have spent a fortune with Doctor Clinton Denton, society's designate plastic surgeon.

Word was that husband Dudley Crenshaw, a real scrooge, had had his tax accountant set up a depreciation schedule for Binky, mixing her name in with his stable of thorough-bred race horses. The IRS thought Binky was just another filly.

Seated across from my little desk, Peter Knapp smiled and said, "You'll do anything for readership—"

"No more boring columns, Mr. Knapp."

He began laughing. "Sorry Patty, but your report of Binky Crenshaw's demise was a doozy. What the hell happened to her?"

"You'll have to wait for the autopsy," I said, not knowing what I was talking about.

Half an hour later a detective Sergeant Johnson called, asking if he come to the paper to question me about the

Crenshaw death. He arrived fifteen minutes later and spent less time than that asking me a few routine questions. Obviously just a formality.

Dudley Crenshaw's doctor didn't think an autopsy was necessary. There was no foul play. They figured she'd died of shock from excess dieting compounded by plastic surgery syndrome.

PATTIE'S CHATTER Nov. 2, 1989 San Francisco Journal

... NO SAD AFFAIR FOR BINKY CRENSHAW'S TRIP TO HEAVEN ... HER ASHES, IN A PRICELESS SIXTEENTH CENTURY CHINESE URN LENT BY GUMP'S ON POST STREET, WERE RAISED ALOFT BY A COLORFULLY CHIC BLUE AND APRICOT STRIPED HOT AIR BALLOON AND SCATTERED OVER THE CHARDONNAY VINEYARDS (BINKY'S FAVORITE WHITE) OF BERINI'S WINERY IN NAPA VALLEY ... (FORGOT TO MENTION BINKY'S TO DIE OVER CREMATORIUM OUTFIT: LYING IN A GUCCI WHITE LEATHER-LINED CASKET, SHE LOOKED STUNNING AND READY FOR A HOT OLD TIME IN HER NEW FIRE ENGINE RED PANTS SUIT BY ADOLFO, TOPPED WITH A DIVINE PAIS- LEY SCARF FROM HERMES NEW SHOP ON UNION SQUARE) ... WHEN THE BALLOON TOUCHED THE GROUND, DUDLEY CRENSHAW (OF THE CALIFORNIA MELON DYNASTY), DRESSED IN A CUTE WESTERN OUTFIT COM- PLETE WITH WHITE STETSON HAT FROM NIE- MAN'S DALLAS, CLIMBED OUT OF THE BALLOON BASKET SHOUTING, "LET THE GAMES BEGIN," AND LIT THE GIANT STACK OF MES- QUITE FOR THE BEEF RIB BARBECUE ... NEENIE

HAVERSTOCK'S LOUIS VUITTON CHAPS WERE
THE TALK OF THE—. . . .

It surprised everyone that Dudley spent so much money
on Binky's memorial service.

The man was so cheap he filled his Rolls Corniche at the
self-service pumps. Friends avoided shaking his hand because it always smelled of unleaded gasoline.

$\triangledown$

The Fish Ball

I HAD A WEEK'S rest after the Crenshaw's barbecue memorial service.

Back at work, I was in the elevator at the Mark Hopkins Hotel zooming up to the ballroom where the "Friends of the San Francisco Aquarium" were staging a $250 a head dinner to raise money for new research on electric eels.

At $250, they could have served abalone, but I thought they'd be sensitive enough not to serve seafood, being "Friends of the Aquarium."

I was wrong, though. All around the room were tanks, more than twenty big tanks, filled with sea water, jammed with lobsters struggling to open their rubber-banded claws.

Hard to believe they were serving lobster at an aquarium benefit, but it figured. Chairwoman Neenie Haverstock was a crazy person about party motifs; it was her life because husband Huntley was never with her. He was too old and couldn't stand social events. Said he preferred being at his Sonoma ranch.

Anyway, Neenie had the whole ballroom in an ocean theme—waiters dressed in yellow slickers with storm hats, tables covered with fish nets, and big fishbowl centerpieces filled with undulating purple squid. Huge speakers around the room were hooked into a continuous tape of roaring surf

13

which I hoped would stop when Ben Benson's local dance band began. The poor band. Already tuning up on the band stand, they were dressed in silly looking sailor suits.

Outside the ballroom guests were chattering away, drinking cocktails from conch shells with green straws that looked like dune grass. Everybody was getting bombed. Drinks were loaded with rum—*Treasure Island* style. The cocktail waiters were wearing eye patches and hooks sticking out of their sleeves, having a dreadful time serving the conch shells. Hors d'ouevres were marinated eel, skewered shrimp, smoked salmon, crab legs and caviar served on tiny pieces of toast shaped like fish. Eight foot sculptured ice statues of a Mermaid and Neptune were beginning to melt all over the floor, which was sprinkled with sawdust, fish market style.

An aging but fairly attractive cocktail pianist was playing "By the Sea," "Red Sails in the Sunset" and other corny salt-water related songs. Our eyes met, in a sly look that said "this is purgatory," and I walked over to say hello.

"Know any ocean type songs?" he asked, with a cute smile.

"How about 'Body and Sole?' " I said.

He got it. I liked him already. He began playing it . . . beautifully. A few bars more and I was his.

Segueing into "How Deep is the Ocean," he asked, "You have to stay here all night?"

"Through dinner at least," I answered, hoping not to lose him forever.

"I'm Rex Murphy. I play downstairs in the cocktail lounge for the late convention drunks. Can you meet me down there for a drink later?"

"I'll be there," I said, almost wetting my pants with excitement and sticking the dune grass straw in my eye.

The dinner speaker was Monterey College's professor of Ichthyology, Gilbert (Gill) Rockdale, who looked and spoke like a dead mackerel. And we could hardly hear the poor man because they hadn't shut off the ocean sound effects tape. Rockdale's big thing was "whales." How we'd be out of whales in 500 years if the Japanese kept harpooning them for their sushi restaurants. I love whales, but the way things were going I figured we'd be out of everything in 500 years, so it wasn't surprising we'd be out of whales, too. Anyway, I couldn't wait to get downstairs to see my piano player.

It was late and Benny Benson's sailor-suited band began playing musical hints to get the crowd moving out . . . "The Party's Over," "Good Night Ladies" . . . The lobster-stuffed, rum-saturated socialites started leaving the ballroom.

I was dying to go downstairs to see Rex Murphy, but I thought it best to finish my job—have my trusty photographer Eddie get a few more shots for Sunday's society page and let the climbers talk to me on their way out. I stayed 'til the ballroom cleared out.

Then it happened again, just like at the Institute of the Third World thing. The cleanup crew found one of the women guests sitting alone at her table, stiff as a board. It was Neenie Haverstock, one of the bluest bluebloods of the city.

$\triangledown$

I Cover the Snowfront

Because of the fuss about Neenie Haverstock I missed my date with Rex, but I knew where he worked.

The next morning Huntley Haverstock helicoptered down from his Sonoma ranch. Much older than Neenie, Huntley had thought all along he'd go first. He couldn't believe it. Except for a mid-life pitstop with Doctor Bogart, Neenie'd never been really sick. (I see Marlon Bogart—society's Mr. Goodwrench—at every ball, and the word is if you want to keep your plumbing don't dance with Marlon.)

Anyway . . . Haverstock—fringy-bald and lunchy around the waist—arrived at the inquiry at 9:30 A.M. I was already there. So were the two Filipino busboys who carried Neenie out and the Haverstock's family physician Dr. Fitzwaterson.

HOMICIDE. That was the little red sign outside the room we entered. Scary.

Mrs. Huntting-Margate wouldn't let me write up Neenie's death in "Pattie's Chatter." It was a "fun" column, she told Peter, and she didn't want it "tainted with unpleasantness." Let the obit take care of it, she told him. She'd hoped I could finesse the inquiry, but I couldn't. The cops had gotten my name.

Two detectives asked us a lot of dumb questions. One looked like Gene Hackman; the other was a big, handsome black man with a gun holster strapped over his shirt. Phones rang constantly. There were lots of little grey metal desks with detective-looking guys sitting at them, all shouting and joking like they do in our city room . . . and laughing a lot. Hard to believe they were in charge of murders.

The detectives filled out forms while a little Chinese guy typed our answers on one of those courtroom machines. I'd expected to be there for hours, but I could see that Lieutenant Kilarney (the guy who looked like Hackman) had more important problems and didn't seem to give a damn about Neenie Haverstock. In less than an hour they let us go without telling us we'd hear from them or anything. I'd had more trouble with parking tickets.

As I was leaving, I heard them making arrangements for an autopsy, and the little Chinese guy asked very casually, like he was inquiring about the weather, if they could have Neenie's organs for the Golden Gate Transplant Bank. Poor Haverstock had such a screaming hangover he'd have given them his own organs to get out of there. He grunted a "yes" and the little Chinese guy banged a few more words on this machine.

The next day I asked Peter if Mrs. Huntting-Margate would at least allow me to write about Neenie's memorial service and she agreed because she expected it to be a chic affair with *everyone* attending.

The Haverstock family was loaded. Huntley's father had invented (word was he stole the idea from a road gang laborer) those little orange reflectors along the edge of freeways, the things that make your tires bop-bop to keep you from driving into the ditch. Last year the Haverstock Road Reminder Corporation celebrated making their one hundred billionth reflector.

Neenie had loved skiing, and had often told Huntley she wanted her ashes scattered in the snow, high in the Sierra's. So Huntley chartered three Amtrak club cars and packed

them with Neenie's mourners and hard core party addicts
who'd have a chance to wear their new ski outfits. Snow was
light in the mountains, too rocky for serious skiing, but
hardly any of her crowd skied anyway.

Peter sent me to cover it.

I'd recently lost a few pounds but still couldn't squeeze
into my old ski clothes. So I figured I'd rent an outfit up there
and put it on my puny expense account.

That evening I wired my column to Peter:

> *PATTIE'S CHATTER from Sugar Bowl San Francisco
> Journal*
>   . . . HAVERSTOCK'S PRIVATE CLUB CARS
> WERE PACKED WITH NEENIE'S FRIENDS HAV-
> ING A HIGH OLD TIME DRINKING MULLED
> WINE, NEENIE'S FAVORITE . . . FROM HUNT-
> LEY'S FABULOUS CHALET, MOURNERS AND
> HAVERSTOCK'S IMMEDIATE FAMILY—WEAR-
> ING DIVINE BLACK BOGNER SKI SUITS, BLACK
> SKI HATS AND GOGGLES (WOMEN'S GOGGLES
> VEILED IN BLACK NET)—TOOK LIFTS TO THE
> TOP. ON THE WAY HUNTLEY SPRINKLED HIS
> BELOVED'S REMAINS FROM ONE OF HER PINK
> NORDICA SKI BOOTS, THE LATEST WITH VEL-
> CRO FASTENERS . . . WAITING AT THE SUMMIT
> WAS THE ENTIRE MORMON TABERNACLE
> CHOIR (HAVERSTOCKS WERE ORIGINALLY SET-
> TLERS OF SALT LAKE CITY) HUMMING NEENIE'S
> FAVORITE, RAVEL'S "BOLERO" . . . CHOIR MEM-
> BERS WORE PINK DOWN JACKETS SPECIALLY
> MADE BY EDDIE BAUER ON POST STREET (BY
> NOW YOU KNOW NEENIE'S FAVORITE COLOR
> WAS PINK) . . . SWINGING RIGHT INTO THE FES-
> TIVITIES WERE BUNKY AND ROD CALTHROP,

COOKIE AND BIFF STONEBANGER, MEG AND
REGGIE VON KELTZ (REGGIE'S DAD WAS PRINCE
GUSTAV VON KELTZ OF AUSTRIA) . . .

That business about Prince von Keltz—Hitler cleaned
him out, and at 79 he's still doorman at the Pierre, wearing
his old military uniform. I hear Meg and Reggie avoid the
Pierre like the plague when they're in New York.

Binky and Neenie were gone . . . out of my boring column
forever. But they died in style—toasting with champagne at
their favorite charity balls. Nice way to go, I thought.

I decided to find Rex. I hoped he remembered me.

Fast Food

I CALLED THE MARK HOPKINS and found that Rex Murphy began playing at 6:00.

No new assignments, so I left the paper early and went home to spruce up before heading over there.

He saw me walk in, but turned his head. I hadn't shown up after the aquarium thing and he was mad. Maybe hurt, not mad. I thought that was a good sign, though. If he hadn't cared, he wouldn't have been upset.

People were gathered at the bar and sitting at the little cocktail tables. Rex was playing Gershwin's "Our Love is Here to Stay," but stopped when he saw me. He gave me that "you're a fine one" look and played a few bars of "Lady is a Tramp" and "Just One of Those Things."

I looked into his eyes and mouthed "Body and Soul." He started playing it immediately. A schmaltzy bit of business but it destroyed me with happiness.

I sat at a small table, sipping a tall Perrier until he finished his cocktail session.

He insisted on taking me to dinner, so we left the Mark Hopkins and drove to his favorite Burger King across town in the Mission district. Rex said he thought I'd like to see the real world for a change, "with me always at fancy balls

20

and dinner parties and things," which sounded to me like a little Irish b.s.

A true gentleman, Rex stood in line for our entrees while I scrambled for an empty table.

In seconds he brought us two giant things with buns the size of throw-pillows, loaded with stuff hanging out the sides.

"A special on Maxi-Whoppers-with-everything," Rex shouted above the crowd. He was all smiles.

So there we were, me all dressed up and he in black tie, sitting among a bunch of seedy looking people devouring Whoppers-with-everything.

Seeing Rex's frayed jacket cuffs, I thought maybe this *was* his real world. Twelve hours a week banging out old show tunes couldn't pay very much.

Rex had that *something* though, and after spending only a few minutes with him I could have been sitting in Maxime's in Paris.

"Just kidding about the real world, Patty. You know—"

"I love it here," I said, tearing a corner off my little foil ketchup packet.

"I feel safer at Jack-in-the-Box, though," he said. "They make everything taste the same."

I laughed, nervously squirting a stream of ketchup from my little packet across the table onto his cummerbund.

"How'd you know I loved ketchup?" he said, wiping off the red blob.

"I'm such a klutz," I said, smiling at his cute remark, which softened my embarrassment.

"But a pretty klutz," he said, squeezing my hand, sending a hot jolt through my chubby little unused body.

"Sorry," I said, realizing he'd grabbed the hand with the messy ketchup packet.

"Maybe we should save a little for the hamburgers." He smiled at me with his green Irish eyes and wiped off his hand.

What a doll. How could I not be falling for him?

"You play the piano beautifully," I said, picking up my throw-pillow-with-everything.

"Never thought I'd get sick of Gershwin and Porter."

"Sounds like *my* job. Same old thing all the time."

"Better than being out of work I guess," he said.

Biting into my giant Maxi-Whopper I damn near dislocated my jaw, recovering just in time to comment. "I don't know about that," I said, feeling a long shred of lettuce drop from my mouth.

Not to hurt Rex's feelings I choked down the rest of the monsterburger. He brought us coffee in styrofoam cups and we chatted quite a while, discovering we had lots in common (except taste in restaurants, but I didn't let on) . . . And I loved his dumb innocent wit that I knew wasn't really dumb or innocent. He seemed to have an honest charm about him. At least I hoped he was honest.

Driving to my apartment in his vintage Camaro, I felt more alive than I'd felt in years. Maybe I'd found a man.

He kissed me goodnight at the door, not asking to come in which I wanted him to do but I didn't encourage it because it was our first date.

It was a sweet kiss. On the lips, but not a heavy, trying-to-turn-me-on, number. Even so I felt that familiar twinge, surprising me because I hadn't twinged in ages.

"May we do this again?" he asked.

I gave him my apartment and office extension number, hoping he'd call the next day which he did, starting a series of fun times together.

$\triangledown$

Buffy's Buffet

THE REALLY BIG DEAL during Christmas season is the Debutante Ball—where society's young ladies are presented to the world to meet young men from the right families.

The number of debs varies each year. Usually about thirty, depending on how many didn't make the cut . . . or made the cut. I forget.

One thing I know—if it's not the biggest party of the year, it's the longest. And the damn things don't really start 'til ten.

On the way in they stamped our hands with that ultra violet stuff used in skating rinks. Unchic, but effective in keeping out the riff raff.

At each place setting were folders listing all the debs' names and their escorts. Some of the escort names killed me, like Lawrence McAdew Taylor-Montague, IV.

After the debutantes were presented, one at a time on a little fairy tale stage, they marched with their escorts under a row of crossed swords (West Point style) while Bernie Hellman's 1940s band played a rousing song about Musketeers. A Nelson Eddy-type number. With such a name, you'd expect something more, but Lawrence McAdew Taylor-Montague, IV turned out to be a scrawny little kid needing Clearasil. I always thought the boys were really cute, though, and had a lot of guts to do it. Next the fathers Strauss-waltzed with their debutante daughters and tears flowed all over the place, including mine. I always cried.

Then everyone joined in the dancing, packing the ballroom floor. The band played old Broadway show tunes. Thousands squeezed together like standing sardines, dancing, chatting, quick-helloing their old friends. The world's record for people saying "nice to see you" was re-established every year at the Deb Ball in the Palace Hotel.

The same old birds I see every year were standing around in their white tie and tails with red ribbons across their chests. The ushers—an honor if you please—Ambassadors of the Ball.

For the young folks they had a half-baked rock band that played numbers popular two years ago. Eardrum-piercing and their beat was a bit off, if you know what I mean. Painful. Rex would have hated it.

Most of the debs, nervous wrecks, had been juicing in their dressing suites and were running around yelling "cosmic" every other word. They looked so young and innocent, so beautiful in their white gowns.

The Deb Ball doesn't raise money for anything. No speakers asking for funds. Just a big blast with enough food and drink to supply St. Anthony's Mission for six months.

Buffy Trexton was the chairwoman. Buffy was another fourth generation San Franciscan. Beautiful and gaunt/chic, Buffy was at every party I covered, always dressed divinely. She must have spent her other life with designers.

At 1 A.M. waiters cleared the quarter-mile of devastated buffet and replaced it with an eighth-of-a-mile of breakfast stuff. Blotters for the boozers. Crepes. Ham steaks. Melon. Strawberries big as tennis balls. Everything. Chefs cooked eggs and pancakes to order on the spot.

Mrs. Huntting-Margate, perpetual Deb Ball committee member, was there so I had to look frantically busy until she left, which was around midnight. But I always stuck around 'til the end anyway doing the picture/name routine for the full page feature on Sunday.

The debs and young people had left, but the old pros, with their frostbitten drink hands, were hanging in.

At 2 A.M. I decided to go, and on the way out stopped at Buffy Trexton's table to tell her how beautiful the party was. She was alone at the table and asked me to join her for a glass of champagne. I thanked her and told her I couldn't. I had to leave to start writing up the party.

Sweet Dreams

"*D*EATH *ALSO MADE ITS debut at last night's Debutante bash. Rederick Trexton found his beautiful socialite wife Buffy stone dead at their dining table in the Palace Hotel ballroom. . . . At 2:10 A.M. this morning, Buffy Trexton, this year's chairwoman of the Debutante Ball . . . .*"

It wasn't a bad dream. I had forgotten to shut off my clock radio alarm when I collapsed in bed about 3 A.M. that morning. It was now 7:30 A.M. and KBCS was blasting the shocking story.

I turned the radio off and put on Channel 10's local morning news. They were showing a videotape of the Palace ballroom swarming with cops and media people as white coat ambulance guys carried poor Buffy—stiff as a board in sitting position—out through the lobby into the SFPD ambulance. Newscaster Myra Bamburger was doing commentary. The reporters and cops had sure gotten there in a hurry. It had happened right after I left.

A taped interview of husband Rederick Trexton followed. He'd left the ballroom for only a few minutes to have the doorman hail his chauffeur. When he returned his wife was dead. Stiff and slightly puffed up like Binky and Neenie.

Then a closeup of the on-the-spot reporter with a staged look of terror on his face: "*I'm Lathrup Truss reporting for*

Channel 10 from the Palace Ballroom where last night Buffy Trexton made her debut into the society of death . . . Sitting straight up in her chair, still clutching her champagne glass, a happy smile on her Patrician face. . . ."

Truss read his cue cards with the compassion of a racetrack announcer.

Family physician Bill Broderick diagnosed it as a massive stroke—same as the others. No foul play.

I dressed quickly and drove to the office.

"This is like Christie's *Ten Little Indians*," I said to Peter.

Peter looked angry. "Mrs. Huntting-Margate called this morning," he said. "Shouting orders for Sunday's deb feature. Lots of pictures, she said. Feature the top families—the Broadweather and Vandercock kids. Better throw in one pretty girl, even if she's not rich—"

"What'd she say about Buffy?" I interrupted.

"I asked her and she said, "Ignore the Buffy Trexton thing."

"Thing?" I said. "The woman died, for Godsakes." I couldn't believe that old bat.

Pink telephone message slips from four television stations and the news/talk radio stations were on my desk. The electronic news vultures had begun circling. Detective Kilarney had also called. Maybe homicide would condescend to take on this case.

I called Kilarney first. He asked if I'd been at the "Debyutrant Event," as he called it. I said yes. He asked if I'd seen Mrs. Buffy there and I said yes. He asked if I'd noticed anyone strange around her table and I said no. Before I could comment, he cut me off without a thank you and hung up. Another routine inquiry for his docket.

The television and radio stations wanted either to interview me for a story or put me on the air with their "journalists." They're all "journalists" now. Even the disc jockeys. I

said I'd need clearance from my editor and would get back
to them, knowing damn well Mrs. Huntting-Margate would
kill the idea.

I went to Peter's office and told him about the stations
calling.

"They want a social angle," I said.

"You know better than that, Patty."

"What'll I tell them?"

"Against the *Journal's* policy."

Peter was still crabby, so I shut up.

I finished the Deb feature, feeling sad for Buffy even
though she'd been sort of a horse's ass.

That afternoon Rex and I went to a bargain matinee at
the Clay. *Au Revoir Les Enfants*. After the movie, we drank
fancy coffee at one of the new million-calorie pastry places
the gays are opening all over Fillmore Street. The pastries
were to die over, but I passed.

Rex looked cute in his navy blue Adidas warmup suit. He
seemed always to be either in black tie or a warm up suit.
People thought he was a health nut, but he never jogged a
step. Just watched football games. *All* of them.

"They're blaming Doctor Denton and Doctor Steinbrenner, the cosmetic surgeons. All three women used them. So
does every aging woman in my column."

"Who's 'they'?", asked Rex, burning his lips on the
steamed Italian coffee.

"The cops. They don't believe it's murder. They've discussed it with the coroner and the city's medical chief.
They're talking about fatal after-effects from all those lift,
tuck and suck jobs."

"Watch your language. You're on Fillmore Street."

I laughed, lifting my cappucino to my lips. "Homicide's
already talked to the staff at Monterey Heights Retreat."

"A drunk drier?"

"Society's fat farm, dear. The ladies all go there to lose

weight. Maybe dry out a little. $750 a day for carrot sticks, flat Perrier and old movies."

Rex rolled his eyes and ordered a brownie.

"All three were thin as sticks," I said. "Died the same way. You can see why the cops like the doctor theory."

"What do they know?" he said, picking up his brownie. I salivated as he devoured it in two bites.

"Lots of Buffy's crowd are too thin and use Denton and Steinbrenner," I said. "But what distinguishes these three is they were all super bluebloods and chairwomen of the balls they died at."

"Tell that one to the cops."

"I did, but they don't listen. Too busy with crack and rape to worry about a few rich ladies dying at parties."

"When's the next ball?" he asked, licking chocolate from his long fingers.

"Next week," I said. "A Symphony benefit in the St. Francis ballroom. Our Symphony orchestra will play Philip Toakhime's new composition and then some dance music. Sort of a Boston Pops thing."

"Toakhime?'

"Billionaire Phil Toakhime, heir to the Toakhime gas pump fortune, practically supports the Symphony and Opera singlehandedly. Phil is a composer manque. More than that, I suppose. He's already composed some things and you know they'll playing anything he writes. He is about thirty and a nice little guy."

My music critic friend, Marv Glickman, told me he sneaked into a rehearsal of "Phil's" first operetta—a bold statement against nuclear energy. Seems this gay Russian hair stylist named Serge is destitute, having lost all his customers who've gone totally bald due to a meltdown in a utility plant near his hometown where he ran his success-ful—thanks to Perestroika—hair salon. Serge sings baritone the first act, changing to tenor in the second act after the meltdown. The format is reminiscent of *A Chorus Line*, except it's gray and downbeat, and the girls and boys in the line are bald as cueballs. To further emphasize the severity of nuclear destruction "Phil's" has the violin, viola, cello and bass players remove the horsehair from their bows and pluck through the whole score. The cast dies on stage in the end except for Serge who is made a non-person and sent to Siberia for blackmarketing hair pieces in Kiev.

The name of the operetta is *The Barber of Chernobyl* and Glickman says it's absolutely dreadful.

I ordered another cappucino, rejecting the pastry. Rex ordered cheesecake.

"You look beautiful," Rex said, putting his hand on mine, not having to reach because the table was the size of a Frisbee.

"Thank you dear," I said, smiling proudly.

We talked more about the dead ladies, and Rex suggested I alleviate my boredom by doing something exciting—secretly investigate the case on my own. He said he'd help me.

"Mrs. Huntting-Margate will fire me on the spot if she finds out."

"She won't find out. Imagine if you solved it," he said. "You'd be the Bernstein/Woodward of the *Journal*. Sneaky journalism. You'd be famous. Television. Books. Attempts on your life. You'd make a fortune."

And I could quit writing my stupid column. I loved this man. I wanted to have his child right there in the Sweet Dreams pastry shop. Thirty-nine's not too old I thought. And so far I'd escaped Goodwrench Bogart.

Interrupting my little day dream, Rex said, "Well, what do you say?"

"I'm scared, but I'll do it. I'll investigate," I said. "And Homicide be damned."

▽

Rex

WE LEFT SWEET DREAMS and walked to Rex's old red
Camaro, the one with the twenty dollar parking ticket under
the windshield wiper. Thirty bucks for coffee and a brownie.

We drove to my place on Green Street, where our beautiful
affair began.

As soon as we got in the door we grabbed each other like
high school kids whose parents had just gone out. We started
tearing off our clothes on the way to the bedroom like we'd
never been laid. My sweater was already off when he picked
me up like Rhett Butler, but he had to put me down when
his warmup pants dropped to his ankles and he couldn't
walk.

We made glorious sweaty love for hours. Absolute heaven.
For fifty, Rex was dynamite. Stiff as old Buffy at the ball. Not
a very nice thought at a time like that, but I couldn't forget
the murders. Yes, I *did* believe they were murders.

Anyway, we had two way sex at its best and I was flying.

Showering together I was embarrassed about my white
flab, but Rex didn't care, particularly while I was soaping up
his member—as Harold Robbins used to refer to them. I
never called them anything to tell the truth. Not that I'd
seen that many, but they were always kind of funny things
to me.

31

Rex was my first real relationship since Charlie, and I was in heaven. A new woman. I began cutting down on food, took a few water pills, and lost five quick pounds. I'm only five-two, so when I lose, you notice it. But we all know the first pounds are the easy ones. All water.

Because of our crazy working hours we saw each other a lot during the day. He lived in the Mission district and I in Cow Hollow just below Pacific Heights. Not exactly shouting distance from each other, so we began having "home and away" games, as my paper's sportswriters would say.

I usually do my own hair, but to expedite my renovation I went all out and had it styled by Pele de Sousa, whom I rarely saw because he was so expensive. Most of the ladies I featured in my column visited his salon regularly at 13 Maiden Lane, known in their crowd as "gossip central." An adorable, charming little man, Pele claimed to be Brazilian, but his envious competitors had spread it around that he sneaked across from his native Tijuana to San Diego and worked at Super Cuts before changing his name and breaking into San Francisco's lucrative hair styling market.

A devout reader of my column, Pele fell all over himself when I arrived. As he softened and frosted my brown curls, already sprinkled with strands of grey—premature of course— he told me how fabulous I looked and proceeded to probe me about Binky, Neenie, and Buffy for his gossip reservoir.

I began to look pretty good if I say so myself, but I figured the remaining pounds'd be tougher to shed. So I kept dieting. Cut down on booze too, but not all the way. Please.

I thought about taking in my dresses, wondering if the old ball gown could weather another alteration.

One night in my apartment Rex and I discussed how I could start my investigation.

"Who's running this Symphony affair?" Rex asked.

"Mimmsy Rittenhouse . . . And I know what you're thinking." Our minds were one.

"She could be next."

"I'll watch her her like a hawk," I said. "Eddie can help me."

"I'm playing late that night or I'd help."

"Don't worry, dear."

Then I told him about the television and radio vultures.

"No supermarket tabloids yet?" Rex said.

"No dear, but the sleazeballs will be here soon. A society mega-scandal's about to explode and you know Mrs. Huntting-Margate will go bananas when our press starts blasting."

He rested his hand on my thigh. Only a warm gesture though, we'd already fooled around enough when he first came over. I put my hand over his.

"The waiters," he said. "Watch the waiters at Mumsy's table. And the people sitting with her."

"You're right dear, I'll watch the waiters. And it's Mimmsy, not Mumsy." I kissed his cheek, of white stubble, as his hand gently wrapped itself around my entire thigh. I could see how he reached a major tenth with no trouble.

Rex had split with is wife ten years ago. After the divorce he moved here from New York to manage KHIP, a weak little FM station that plays Gillespie, Basic, Miles Davis, and the rest of them. Good station except for the discordant stuff by the new whacked-out jazz "innovators."

A couple of years ago an Iranian bought the station and Rex was history. Being "overqualified"—headhunter for "too old"—he couldn't get a decent job, so he brushed up on his piano, which he'd played semi-professionally in college, got a few party gigs, and a few months before we met landed a job at the Mark Hopkins bar. A living.

As we talked an idea hit me: Table seatings were usually pre-arranged. Could I get a list of the guests who'd sat with the three ladies?

"Great idea," Rex said, looking at his Timex.

"Time goes by too fast when we're together," I said.

"'Specially in bed," he said, kissing my cheek.

We got up at 9 the next morning, early for us. I hadn't written my column yet, and Peter would be waiting for me.

Rex and I had already left reserve underwear and stuff at each others' apartments, so before he put on his warm-up suit I gave him clean boxer shorts, thankful to God he didn't wear those ball-holder things like women's panties.

He tried shaving with my armpit razor and it damn near disfigured his face, so he skipped shaving. His stubble was mostly white anyway so you didn't notice it. His birthday was coming up and I planned to give him a Norelco Cordless to keep in my bathroom.

I got dressed—thrilled that my old plaid skirt was feeling looser around the waist—kissed Rex goodbye and tore out the door.

When I got to the office I looked at my notes. "Dance with the Symphony" was Friday, in three days. Except for Toakhime's music, it could be fun. But I was afraid for Mimmsy Rittenhouse—chairmwoman, rich, gaunt/chic and from one of the city's most royal families.

▽

H - M

H-M ALWAYS DEALT DIRECTLY with Peter, my editor. I hardly ever saw her, but she was asking for me when I got in.

Waiting outside her office I was a wreck. Her giant oak door with a brass plate saying "Publisher" looked like the entrance to a fort. But as heavy as the door was, I could hear a hot argument going on, though I couldn't catch the words.

Minutes later a red-faced, overweight, middle-aged guy stormed out—Rudolph, Junior, the old bat's son. Junior was editor-in-chief and everyone knew he was the one who really ran the paper. And the word was that if it weren't for mother, he'd have dumped my column long ago. I couldn't really blame him.

My turn to go in. My mouth was bone dry and my tongue was stuck to the roof of my mouth.

"Sit down my child," she said.

I sat in an obese, brown leather chair in front of a desk the size of an aircraft carrier. Her new custom wheelchair's mahogany headrest towered above her puffy grey/blond hair. On the headrest was a gold Huntting-Margate family crest which I'd heard was on everything she owned, including her toilet seat covers.

She looked like an ancient W.C. Fields in drag and her

voice was old and phlegmy. Hanging from her mouth, making her look like those tough guys who shoot pool, was a short, non-filter Camel, and her left eye was squeezed shut from the smoke.

"I must commend you for the recent improvement in your column," she rasped.

With God's help my tongue snapped loose. "Thank you Mrs. Huntting-Margate," I said, having no idea what she was talking about.

"Makes it easier for them to pick out their names." Her voice fluttered like a whoopy cushion.

"So happy you—"

"That's all they give a damn about anyway."

Then I realized what she was talking about. A few weeks ago I'd asked the typesetter to set the names of people in my column in bold face type. Peter, my editor, loved the idea which I sort of stole from a *New York Post* columnist.

"Simple ideas are usually the best," I said humbly. "And it didn't add any cost." My mouth was a blotter.

"Maybe a tad more ink," she chuckled, setting off a major death-rattling coughing fit.

"A glass of water, perhaps?" I said, hoping I could get one for myself.

"Thank you my child, I'm fine." She needed oxygen, not water.

She couldn't have called me up here to talk about bold face type, for Godsakes.

"Pity about our three lovely ladies," she said quietly so as not to arouse the Camel-induced polyps on her voice box.

Here it comes, I thought.

"What do you think Patty? You were at all three affairs with them." In respect for the departed, she'd removed the cigarette from her thin blue lips.

"The police think it's some sort of medical problem," I said. "Excessive dieting, faulty cosmetic surgery." I wasn't about to give her my real thoughts.

"I asked what *you* thought, Patty," she said, sounding like Snow White's wicked queen with a Hepburn accent.

"I'm inclined to agree with the police, Mrs. Huntting-Margate."

"Call me 'H-M', dear."

Suddenly I was one of the privileged. What did she want from me?

"Let's hope they prove the medical theory soon," she said. "It's been damned disruptive for our little group."

Anything to keep her social set pristine. H-M was about to tell me not to screw around with the situation.

"I know how curious you newspaper reporters are, Patty dear, and I can't blame you, but I do hope you'll just forget these unfortunate incidents and let things take their course."

She lit another Camel, flicking a kitchen match with her thumbnail, singeing the stray hairs that had escaped her spray lacquer.

"I'll just keep doing my job, Mrs. Hunt—M-H, I mean H-M."

"I shall write a note to your editor, recommending you for an increase in salary for your innovative 'bold face' format."

Now I could buy that Lear Jet I always wanted.

She smiled as if she were about to push me into the oven with Hansel and Gretel, then spun around in her wheelchair and picked up the phone, indicating that our meeting was over and I could leave.

I left, heading for the nearest water cooler.

$\bigtriangledown$

Too Many Notes

R EX DEFINES A TRUE gentleman as a man who owns an accordian but doesn't play it. Good thing he wasn't here because roaming among the cocktailers outside the St. Francis Hotel ballroom a curly-haired Italian accordionist was wheezing "Lady of Spain," "Kitten on the Keys," and other dreadful numbers.

Junior Leaguers with balloons tied to their waists were selling drink tickets and hustling sweepstakes chances for prizes donated by companies needing publicity.

We expected some sort of surprise because the ballroom doors were still shut.

It was Toakhime's big night. His first symphony. Probably cost him a half million in contributions to get it played, but at least "Phil's" was doing more than just going to parties.

I saw my paper's music critic, Marvin Glickman. Tough for Marv to keep any journalistic integrity, I thought. If he panned Toakhime's composition, symphony contributions would dry up and "H-M" could get rough.

Marv whispered in my ear. "It's gotta be better than 'Barber of Chernobyl'."

"What's the name of tonight's disaster?" I asked.

"Don't know," Marv whispered. "So hush, hush, they kept me out of rehearsal."

I had the guest list for Mimmsy Rittenhouse's table and managed to get a seat two tables away. My photographer Eddie promised to stay close to me and keep his eyes peeled. I looked forward to a nervous night.

The light began flicking on and off. Two bellhops opened the giant folding doors and the mob of chatting drinkholders poured into the ballroom.

What a sight it was. Spanning the entire length of the ballroom was a huge Golden Gate Bridge in gold sequins appliquéd onto a blue velvet curtain they must have borrowed from Radio City Music Hall. Hundreds of silver sequined musical notes that looked like little people were jumping off the sequined bridge, with some already splashing into the white-capped, green sequined water.

Above the bridge in big flashing light bulb letters it said: "SUICIDE SUITE," a symphony by PHILIP TOAKHIME.

Loud oohs and aahs burst from the crowd, already in good shape from patronizing the balloon girls.

On a huge stage in front of the bridge the white-tied symphony musicians waited for Toakhime.

The crowd settled, already into their Bocci Vineyards donated wine, and Mimmsy Rittenhouse walked out onto the stage in her $900,000 outfit, diamond tiara included, to thank us for coming and ask for more money for the symphony, which was always broke. She read the list of the evening's benefactors, including Sophie and Morris Jacobs who'd donated two thousand pounds of sequins shipped from his uncle's button and trim operation in Manhattan.

I saw H-M in her portable wheelchair sitting at Mimmsy's table. First time she'd come to an event in a wheelchair. I figured whatever she had, it was getting worse.

Finally Mimmsy introduced Toakhime, a cute little guy with lots of black curly hair who looked funny in tails because he was so short. He tapped the stand with his baton and the musicians poised for the attack.

For the longest time I thought they were still tuning up,

then realized they were well into the first movement. The musicians seemed to be in pain, the cello players sawing so fast their arms were blurred. Even the cymbal player was busy as hell, crashing his things together like crazy. And I knew the tympani guy was headed for tennis elbow.

Toakhime was orgasmic, smiling, whipping his baton around as if he were dueling Errol Flynn. With a goosing motion, his left hand signaled to play louder and faster. It sounded like Wozzek played sideways, and so loud the speaker fronts were bulging.

To make it worse my table was a few feet from the stage.

At one precious moment they stopped playing and the crowd, who'd finished every bottle of wine in sight by then, began to applaud. But it was only the end of another movement.

Toakhime's face and shirt front were soaking wet as he hit the home stretch. Finally it ended. Toakhime and the musicians bowed, and the crowd screamed, thankful it was over.

No encore, thank God. The musicians couldn't have taken it, and it was 10 o'clock, with no dinner yet.

During dinner I figured the phantom might do his number on Mimmsy's food or drinks. It had to be something taken internally. Binky, Neenie and Buffy had had no needle marks or other marks. Eddie and I kept watching Mimmsy's table but suddenly the room went pitch black. We couldn't see a thing, except smokers lighting cigarettes.

When the waiters lit candles I could see around me pretty well. Well enough to see that Mimmsy Rittenhouse was not at her table.

In five minutes the lights came back on. Word was that Toakhime's "Suicide Suite" had shorted out the electrical system.

The noise level climbed back to party volume and I saw Prudence Lansdale-Chase and her new husband arrive and sit down at Mimmsy's table. Lucky things had missed the music. Mimmsy and Prudence had been dear friends for years and it made no difference to Mimmsy that Prudence— a regally beautiful red head and well preserved for fifty something—had married a black doctor.

A bit of a scandal that, but San Francisco society is more forgiving than the East. In Philadelphia she'd have been a nonperson. Imagine a name like Prudence Jabbar-Lamumba. And his first name, dear God, was Boolabar. Sounded like a Stanford football cheer. But everyone seemed to like Booly. Good looking dude about 35. Built like the guy who fought Rocky, but bigger.

Fascinating story, how they met. For two years after his stroke poor old Tucker Lansdale-Chase—twenty years older than Prudence—had been under 24-hour care in a chic hospital in Sonoma. About a year ago husband Tucker drooled his last drop and Prudence was free as a bird with millions in tax-free bonds to play with.

I remember featuring Prudence in my column when she left on a trip to Africa ". . . flying off in her Ralph Lauren/Banana Republic ensemble, complete with Gucci bandolier thrown over her shoulder . . ."

On a safari in Kenya and side trips to lesser known spots she met Boolabar, who must have filled more than Tucker's shoes because we'd never seen Prudence happier.

Nasty gossip had it that Booly's dad was a tribal witchdoctor and had saved enough shrunken heads and rhino horns to send his son to college and med school.

When they met, Doctor Jabbar-Lamumba was conducting research at Bayanga Medical Institute, the Mayo Clinic of Chad. His project concerned sex habits and the life expectancy of Africans north of the Equator, funded by a United States grant. (Seems to me sending food would have been more helpful, but what did I know?)

Anyway, Pru and Booly were happy as clams living in their Nob Hill co-op and spending winters at the Jabbar-Lamumba family vacation compound on Lake Chad at the

Nigerian border. Though Booly had been drummed out of "Top Tribes" (their sort of Social Register) for marrying a white woman, his parents accepted Prudence with open arms, allowing her to eat with them in their dining room.

As I turned away from nodding to Prudence, I saw that Mimmsy hadn't disappeared. I was so relieved. She'd been with the musicians and was back on stage telling us the Symphony orchestra would play dance music conducted by Bjorg Varner of the Stockholm Symphony. Bjorg was in San Francisco for a year on an exchange program sponsored by Absolut. Smooth stuff, but I couldn't afford it.

A nice evening for a change, but I was still worried sick about Mimmsy.

Eddie kept snapping pictures, checking in with me every few minutes. I noticed H-M had left—probably disgusted because she couldn't dance anymore.

I stayed 'til the very end and saw that all tables were empty. I saw no stiff little ladies. The phantom had missed. Or maybe Mimmsy wasn't the target.

Before the cleanup crew came in I walked over to check out Mimmsy's table, and near the centerpiece of flowers I found something odd. Something I thought I should take with me.

$\triangledown$

Everybody's in the Act

THE FLUTED CHAMPAGNE GLASS hadn't been used. Bone dry. But in the bottom of it was a little yellow thing, like a stick. I inverted the glass and let the thing fall onto the table. Could've been a perfume sample, but I didn't think so. I picked it up with a Kleenex, wrapped it and put it in my purse.

At home I unwrapped it. It looked like a fat, see-through toothpick. Pale yellow. I put it in a white saucer on the counter next to the stove. Could be dangerous—poison maybe—so I didn't touch it with my bare fingers. Much too late to call Rex. I'd tell him about it in the morning.

Too wound up to sleep, I turned on the television set and found a high-numbered UHF channel was still on the air, repeating one of those dreary local panel shows seen Saturday mornings before the cartoons. "Face Your Something" or "This is Your City"—the ones nobody watches. This had Chinese subtitles.

Featured guest was Sal Mancotti, president of our Board of Supervisors. The host was that old political analyst, Foster Fagan, with the hair comb that looks like a Pope's beanie.

Rex knew Mancotti. He was always at the Mark Hopkins bar, asking Rex to play "That's Amore."

Our Board of Supervisors is a joke. Khadafy could run the city better. The Board of Supervisors is determined to turn San Francisco into one big movie set. They're chasing business out in droves. The Navy's gone, no more shipping, and our piers are turning into flea markets. They want bridge tolls raised to twenty bucks to keep cars out of the city. And they just told the Olympic committee they were too macho for our town.

To make matters worse nobody ever sees our new Mayor Skiathos.

Good God, Mancotti was talking about Binky, Neenie and Buffy. Foster Fagan hadn't even approached the subject and Mancotti had his big nose in it.

"We're concerned about our citizens' health," Sal said.

Sal Mancotti'd been running for mayor since birth. Always plugging away. Last year Skiathos creamed him in the primary eighty percent to twenty percent.

"I know that, Supervisor Mancotti, but—" Foster Fagan said.

The subject of the interview, by the way, was *Why Close Our Libraries?*

"Those three women, for instance," Mancotti said. "We're looking into why they died. We know they were in hotels when it happened."

Foster couldn't get in a word.

"Our board just put Binky and the other dead ladies on our agenda. We'll fund another study on asbestos and fluoride in our hotels. Our citizens deserve solutions to these health problems, Fagan."

"But would asbestos zero in on just three women, Supervisor Man—?"

"Gay baths," Sal snapped, ignoring Foster and looking sternly into the camera. "Our study on gay baths proved us right on that one."

"Why are you closing more libraries, Superv—?"

"Public toilets. Remember our study on public toilets,

Foster? We sent Sarah Goldman to Paris, best public toilet city in the world."

"Wouldn't it serve the public better to fund libraries instead of toilets, Supervisor Mancotti?"

"Our dream is a toilet on every corner, Fagan. Sarah's got Walter Landor working on designs as we speak."

Foster Fagan's frustration showed, but he kept his journalistic cool.

"Getting back to those three rich broa—women, Foster. . . . Wine. More tax on wine, people will drink less, be healthier."

"Paris has good public libraries, too, Superv—"

"Nobody reads anymore, Fagan. They watch televison. 'Sesame Street's' where it's at. My kids learned half the alphabet on that show."

"There's more reading now than ever, Supervisor Manc—"

"Why waste money on books? We need a gay softball stadium for the Castro Caballeros. Housing for the poor. Heard about our study on fog? We now know people are poorer in foggy sections. The rich aren't in the fog. We've got to equalize that situation."

Foster Fagan then introduced Ms. Fannie Doerflinger, head of SOB (Save Our Books), formerly of SOW (Save Our Whales), who gave a long diatribe on illiteracy. Mancotti kept interrupting, talking about "doing more with less."

Before I turned the damned thing off, Sal Mancotti said his Board would put pressure on the police and health department about Binky, Neenie and Buffy "so this dreadful thing couldn't happen to more of our citizens through neglect of city health standards." Mancotti would talk about anything for publicity.

In seconds I fell asleep, and woke up at 7:30, too early to call Rex.

I went to the kitchen to make coffee and check the little thing. The dish had a big drop of yellow fluid with a little white stuff mixed in. Some investigator. I'd let my evidence melt.

I had to call Rex.

"Rex? Patty. Good news. Mimmsy Rittenhouse left the ball on her own."

"On her own what?" he mumbled. The poor dear was half asleep.

"I didn't see her leave, but she must be alive. She could have got it though, even though I watched her like a hawk."

"Got what? It's only eight o'clock. What the hell are you talking about?"

"I found this thing."

"Call me later."

"Could be the phantom's weapon."

"What is it?"

That got his heart started.

"A little stick, fatter than a toothpick. Like one of those tiny Christmas tree lights, only longer. Looks like pale yellow Jello."

"Sounds like an old Beatles tune."

"Please."

"Don't touch it with your bare hands."

"It melted."

"Nothing left?"

"A drop of yellow liquid."

"Be right over."

I turned on Channel 6, Traffic News from Helicopter Six. The woman with the constipated smile was yelling about bridge tie-ups, rear-enders and acid spills. Then four commercials in a row—*Kellogg's* cancer free bran flakes, *Weight Watchers'* lasagna, cholesterol-free *Quaker Oats* and the Neptune Cremation Society.

Then, my god, anchorwoman Myra Bamburger came on and interviewed Lieutenant Kilarney about "society's triple tragedy." Kilarney said there was no foul play. He talked about Doctors Denton and Steinbrenner and how our health department officials had investigated them. Kilarney swore their treatments were linked to the deaths.

The police were stalling the press, the public, City Hall and Mancotti's board of parasites. Denton and Steinbrenner would probably go bankrupt, and cosmetic surgery would be blackballed. A moratorium on refound youth. Panic by the Bay.

Rex was at the door. I knew his knock.

"Come in my love."

Looking divine in his Herschel Walker black and red Adidas warm-up suit, he leaned down to kiss me. Way down. Rex was a foot taller than I. He hadn't shaved. A bit dated, he called it his "Miami Vice" look.

He'd heard the same Kilarney interview on his car radio.

"Look for the world series of malpractice suits," I said.

"Not if you get the phantom. Let's see your thing," he said, with a dirty smile. That's all Rex ever thinks about.

We went to the kitchen.

"No wonder it melted," he said, "It's touching the top of the stove."

"The stove hasn't been on—"

"The pilot lights keep it warm. Feel."

I put my hand on top of the stove. Warm.

"Whatever that stuff is, it melts easily."

"What do we do?" I asked.

"Put it in the refrigerator and let it harden."

I carefully put it in the freezer next to the Lean Cuisine.

"While we're waiting," Rex said. "Let's go in the bedroom and see if I can—"

"Don't say it," I said, grabbing his hand and leading him out of the kitchen.

After fooling around waiting for the thing to harden in the refrigerator, we fell asleep for an hour. I needed it. Hardly any sleep last night and Rex is like being in bed with an exercycle.

10 A.M. Shower time and then to work. I let Rex sleep.

Before leaving I opened the refrigerator. It had hardened but the "case of the melted yellow Jello" would have to wait if I wanted to keep my job. I was scheduled to cover a luncheon called "Mission: Transition."

∇

Dilemma

"MISSION TRANSITION" WAS SPONSORED by Grandame
Meloney Bluxome whose grandfather made his fortune selling picks to the forty niners—the miners, not the team. Mrs.
B., a sentimental caring old soul, was always reaching out
to the downtrodden and misfits. She was in the right city.

The event, held in the Castro Theater lobby, benefited the
new Psychiatric Clinic for Ambivalent Transsexuals.

What a nutty looking crowd. All in evening gowns, like a
men's club in drag for their annual hi-jinks. Eddie was
having so much fun he ran out of film.

White wine was flowing. So was marijuana, and I could
never stand that smell.

Doctor Hubert Short, head of the new clinic, had run
Bellevue's disgenderophobia clinic in New York. He looked
like Joan Rivers with a crew cut.

The costume party quieted down to let Mrs. Bluxome
introduce Short, who then spoke at length about the transsex-
ual dilemma, relating his own painful emotional experiences.

He'd brought along two of his cured patients—a stunning
blond in a Fila tennis dress and a brunette in a Degas ballet
outfit. The ballet dancer needed improvement. She had cute
little boobs but telltale knotty knees, and the beard showed
through the makeup. They both spoke of their wonderful

49

new lives in rather deep voices, a problem Doctor Short was
working on.

They could carry helium balloons I thought, smiling at
my little joke.

Short's solution was to tighten their vocal cords, demon-
strating his idea on a cello, bowing the high and low strings.

A burst of applause and a few soprano screams.

After the buffet everyone swished into the theater to see
Short's new documentary. Not for me thank you. I sneaked
off.

I wrote my column—which wasn't easy given the subject
matter—gave it to Peter and went home.

That evening the *Examiner's* headline read: "Are Denton
and Steinbrenner Out After Three Strikes?" Inside the
paper Hyman Gold's column, *Hy's Society*, featured photos
of the three dead socialites.

Rex came over the next morning about 10 and wanted to
fool around.

"We've got to talk about our case," I said.

"Later my love."

He had that look.

"Am I just a sex object? Don't you ever think of me as a
human being?" I asked.

"Yes, but not often," he said, smiling the smug way he
does.

He caught my hand as I was playfully about to slap his
face, grabbed me in his arms and I was his.

"But it's hardened," I said, referring to the melted thing.

"Not yet," he said.

We showered off our fun and put on warm-up suits—he
had me wearing them now—and went into the kitchen.

"I'm thinking of you as a human being this very moment," he said.

I got on tippy toes and kissed the big lug, giving him a soft
knee to the groin.

He opened the refrigerator. "We did it," he said. "We'll put it in a little jar or something."

"Want some eggs and bacon?" I asked.

"Got any danish?"

Rex eats junk food, never exercises and looks in better shape than those sweating clowns you see running all around the city.

I warmed a big wedge of Weight Watchers crumb cake and made fresh coffee.

"As I tried to say before you sexually assaulted me, we've got to talk about our case."

"So talk. Any ideas?"

"What would Margaret Truman do?" I said.

He laughed. "She'd be sprinkling suspects through her pages. Maybe we should list suspects—who'd do it? And why? What's the motive?"

"How very detective," I said.

"But we're going at this ass backwards. Let's find out first what that stuff is. It's probably the weapon and by now it's contaminated your Lean Cuisine."

"Miss Marple would take it to a chemist."

"And have it analyzed."

"That's it," I said.

$\triangledown$

The Marvin Connection

I WALKED TO UNION Street where Marvin was hanging on with white knuckles to keep his little drug store. Hong Kong money was buying every little old building on the street and rents were exploding. New restaurants and dress shops opened and closed every other week. To make ends meet, the last little grocer on the street was charging like Tiffany's—like cat food a dollar fifty a can. Seven-Eleven was selling Godiva chocolates. It was that kind of a street.

Marvin called his store "Marvin's" and ran it all by himself. As I walked in, the little brass bell on top of his door tinkled—a nice touch in this microchippy world. Marvin waved at me and smiled. He had on his old white coat with a thousand pencils in the top pocket and was on the phone as usual, like all pharmacists.

Before asking where I could find a chemist to analyze the stuff, which was at home in an old Valium bottle in my refrigerator, I bought a couple of things to give Marvin a little business: Vidal Sassoon mousse, which I'd never used pre-Rex, and desert-tan panty hose.

Marvin rang up the sale and I asked who he'd recommend.

"Stanley Herkimer does that," Marvin said. I could hardly see his eyeballs his glasses were so thick. "If he's still alive. He has a loft on Howard Street."

"Is he in the phone book?"

"Calls himself Bayview Chemists. Want me to phone him for you?"

"Fabulous," I said.

After I got home I dialed Bayview Chemists. The crackling sound wasn't a bad connection—it was Mr. Herkimer and he knew who I was. We made an appointment for the next morning at 9.

Pinkus Maximus

DON'T ASK ME WHY but the persistent little red light on my answering machine intimidates me. I can't stand answering machines, but I needed one for my job.

I rewound it, turned to "Play Messages" and after the beep a rough voice with a thick Bronx accent came on. (Rex had taught me how to tell Brooklyn, Bronx, Jersey, Long Island and Manhattan accents). "Maximillian Pinkus from the *National Intruder* calling. Please call me at 386-9000, room 872. Important." Another beep and, "Hello Miss Nottingham. Benny Barnes of the *Star* calling us from Los Angeles. Love to hear from you. Please call us toll free 800-383-STAR."

Sleazeball time.

I called Pinkus. The Hyatt Regency operator answered, connected me with room 872 and Maximillian gave his spiel about wanting to use my name for a social angle story. They already had a title: *Dance Macabre at Frisco Balls—Charity Chicks Check Out.* Society scribe, Patty Nottingham, tells her story.

Good God.

"I'm sorry, Mr. Pinkus, but I must decline."

"I've heard that before, Miss Nottingham. You'll change your mind when you hear my deal."

54

"It's against the *Journal's* policy, Mr. Pinkus."

"Call me Max. Against policy to have dinner with me, Miss Nottingham?"

"Thank you so much but I can't tonight."

"Got reservations at Masa's."

"Please Mr. Pinkus."

"I'll send a limo for you."

"I'm going to bed early."

"What a shame. So what'll I do with all this money I've got for you?"

"Have a swinging night on the town, Mr. Pinkus. Goodnight."

He was a persistent creep. Imagine trying to buy me. I wondered how much it was.

I wanted a quiet evening for a change. I'd read a little. And the hell with Barnes and his *Star.*

But as my grandmother used to say, there was no rest for the weary. At 10 o'clock somebody leaned on my buzzer.

I walked to the speaker button and pressed it. I wasn't surprised.

"Maximillian Pinkus of *The Intruder.* I thought if you couldn't sleep, we could talk."

I kept cool because you can't get rough with these guys.

"Sorry Mr. Pinkus, I told you—"

"Call me Max." The speaker cackled over his gross voice. "We'll make you famous, Miss Nottingham. May I call you Patty?"

I prayed no one in the lobby was hearing us.

"The lead story, Patty. Life size shot of your pretty face on the cover. That's only the beginning. Everybody'll want your story—"

Sure, I thought, and everyone in San Francisco would want me in court. And how did he know I had a pretty face?

"My publisher forbids me, Mr. Pinkus—"

"Are the Huntting-Margate snobs against freedom of the press f'chrissake?"

"Good night, Mr. Pinkus. Thank you again."

Before I could shut off the intercom, he said, "The contract's in your mailbox, Miss Nott—"

How could I not go down to the mail box? I slipped on my warmup suit, hurried down to the lobby and pulled out the fat white envelope. Inside was a contract on an *Intruder* form and clipped to it a note in loud handwriting said:

"MISS NOTTINGHAM:
SUGGEST YOU SIGN THE ATTACHED.
WE EXPECT TO FEATURE FRISCO STORY NEXT
WEEK.
MAXIMILLIAN PINKUS"

I flicked through the contract to see how much. $25,000. It would take me a year to make that at the chintzy *Journal*.

$\triangledown$

Suspicions

Next MORNING I TOOK the Valium bottle with the stuff in it to Stanley Herkimer. Driving over I couldn't stop thinking about that creep Pinkus.

Herkimer's place was in a wrecked old building at 66 Howard Street where I got a parking place right in front and the meter was broken with a note already on it. Heaven.

I found a rusty metal door with a faded Bayview Chemists sign screwed to it. Figuring the rusted doorbell button hadn't worked for years, I knocked.

Herkimer had on a grey sweatshirt like Einstein used to wear and long grey crinkly hair hanging from the sides of his bald head like a Victorian lampshade. He didn't look at me, just turned around and shuffled back to his mad scientist work table, and I followed. He walked bent over as if he were looking through a microscope. Across the room I saw a filthy unmade cot against an old brick wall, and I figured he lived in that black-and-white horror movie set.

The place gave me the "guilts"—as if I'd been sent there for an abortion or some other nasty thing.

Finally he looked up at me with a white pruney face that had probably never been outside his room.

"Mr. Marvin told me about you," he said. Even in person Herkimer sounded like a bad phone connection.

I handed him my little bottle and he said, "You need more Valium? Go back to Marvin."

I explained it was an old prescription bottle and that inside it was the substance I wanted analyzed.

He took it from me, opened it and got his tweezers. I told him how it had melted and to be careful.

He stared at me as if I were a stupid ass and mumbled something about viscosity. "Minimum charge hundred fifty for three hours work. Any longer, fifty an hour more." He'd run out of breath and wheezed in some new air.

"That's expensive for a working girl," I said, giving him my coy smile.

"You're not buying Valium, lady."

"Please call as soon as you're finished and I hope you can hold it to a hundred and fifty." I gave him my phone number.

"For a friend of Marvin's I'll do it."

My hours were weird. If I worked a night party, I was off the next morning and went to work in the afternoon. If I worked day things, I was off evenings. Sometimes I worked both day and night events. I never knew. As long as I covered everything and wrote my column I was pretty much on my own.

At 4 o'clock Rex came to my apartment. I made coffee and we sat on the couch to discuss the murders. At least I thought they were murders.

First I told him about the tabloids calling and how Pinkus had harrassed me.

"You can't win with those scumbags," he said.

That icky word had recently been introduced into Northern California by transplanted Easterners. I asked Rex to please not use it.

"Sorry love, but that's what they are."

"Parasites would be better."

"I'll buy that. But stay away from the sonsabitches."

I showed him the contract.

"Twenty-five. That's big time. Know what the scum—bastards are doing?"

"Offering a fee for my interview, that's what they're doing."

"So they can say they made the effort. They'll print a story using your name anyway. They may even send you a check without your agreement."

"Tempting, but I'd tear it up."

"They don't give a shit."

"I could sue them."

"Know someone at the Cryogenic Society?"

"Come on—"

"They could freeze you 'til your trial comes up in the year 3,000."

"Let's drop it and talk about something more horrible," I said.

"When do you get the analysis?"

I wanted to say "where do I get a hundred and fifty bucks?", but I wouldn't bother Rex about money. What could a cocktail pianist make?

"Could hear this afternoon," I said. "But I doubt it. Herkimer's older than God."

"Not too swift."

"A banana slug moves faster."

"If that stuff's poison and the little sticks were in the ladies' champagne glasses, how come they didn't see it?"

"It was too late. They were probably loaded by then and didn't notice it. Be tough to see it in the dim lighting, and those fluted glasses are deep."

"So let's list the suspects," he said. "And possible motives." I wondered if Rex was ill. He hadn't asked me to bed yet. He had a pencil and yellow pad on his lap.

"We'll start with the people who sat with our victims the nights they were found dead. I have the seating arrangements for Neenie and Buffy's tables, but it was so long ago I don't have Binky's table. Probably the same though."

"So let's have what you've got," Rex said.

"Ready? First Neenie's table: Mrs. Huntting-Margate and escort Lamar Philbin; Doctor and Mrs. Boolabar Jabbar-Lamumba—"

Rex did a take on that one and asked me to spell it.

". . . Mr. and Mrs. Rodman Rittenhouse—that's Mimmsy . . . and of course poor Neenie Haverstock, with Gardner, her bachelor brother."

"Where was Neenie's husband?" Rex asked.

"Huntley avoids these things. He's usually at his ranch."

"I don't blame him."

"Now Buffy's table: Rodman and Mimmsy, again; Mrs. Huntting-Margate and escort Lamar Philbin—"

"Who's Lamar Philbin?" Rex asked.

"Our city's emerging young fashion designer, *dahling*. Gay as a hummingbird in honeysuckle. Moving along . . . the Jabbar-Lamumba's, Dudley Crenshaw and his date, Shotsie Fenner—"

"Didn't take Dudley long," Rex said, smiling.

"And, of course, Buffy Trexton and husband Rederick."

"What about Neenie?"

"She was dead by then. Her ashes were on a ski slope."

"Sorry. So that's Buffy's table. Mostly the same people at both tables."

"Not unusual, they're all dear friends and get together at these things. Most tables have their same little groups of old friends."

"So why the hell would any of them want to kill their friends?" Rex asked, arranging his "Motives" column on the pad.

"Let's review how our three victims were found," I said. "They were all sitting up, smiling, toasting with their champagne. All stiff as a board and a bit puffed up, like they hadn't taken their water pills. And it happened after dinner when people were dancing and drinking."

"And you were present when the cleanup crew found them?"

"Not when they discovered Buffy," I said. "Heard about her the next morning. Remember?"

Rex scribbled my name in his "suspect" column.

"What are you doing?" I said.

"Y'never know," Rex said, kissing my cheek.

Then he began jotting down our thoughts, suspicions and possible motives:

1. Mrs. Huntting-Margate—Why so adamant about not writing up the deaths in PATTIE'S CHATTER? Why did she warn Patty that day in her office? Was she terminal from smoking those no-filter Camels? Was she getting even with youth and beauty because she was over the hill and not able to dance anymore?

2. Lamar Philbin—Was he in a snit because society had scorned his gowns? Did H-M use him as her assassin, promising him gown business from her rich friends?

3. Prudence Jabbar-Lamumba—Had she contracted some awful disease in the Third World that had passed on to our three susceptible, undernourished ladies? Or did Prudence suspect that old Tucker Lansdale-Chase had been fooling around with the three ladies before his stroke? Is that why Tucker couldn't get it up for Prudence all those years?

4. Doctor Boolabar Jabbar-Lamumba—Was Booly really a witch doctor like his father? A terrorist for the Third World?

5. Dudley Crenshaw—Binky'd been registered as one of his thoroughbred race horses. Was there a big insurance policy? What about Neenie and Buffy's husbands? Were their wives heavily insured? Weren't these guys rich enough without insurance money? Were they all sick of going to dances?

6. Shotsie Fenner (Dudley Crenshaw's new girlfriend)— Could she have helped Dudley get rid of Binky? But she'd have no reason to murder Neenie and Buffy . . . unless we see her dating Huntley and Rederick.

7. Mimmsy Rittenhouse—Assume she's still alive and well, having left the Symphony affair that night. The only thing that makes her a suspect is that we know she sat with Neenie and Buffy the nights of their deaths, and probably sat with Binky too.

8. Rod Rittenhouse—Harmless, except he's a registered Democrat.

"That's about it," Rex said.

"Wait dear. Maybe one more: Junior. I have a strange feeling about Junior."

"Junior?"

"Mrs. Huntting-Margate's son Rudolph. He really runs the paper. Bitter man. Always fighting with his mother. A big liberal and hates his mother's crowd."

"Gotta watch those liberals. Maybe he'll kill his mother, too. I'll put him down."

Rex put his pad on the coffee table. "So there's the list," he said. "Maybe we're kidding ourselves. For all we know it could be a crazed waiter sick of his job. And we don't even know what that stuff is you found. Could be a harmless thing that fell out of the flower arrangement. They always have flowers on the tables don't they? Remember in botany class about stamens and cross-pollenization and pistils?"

He put his warm, long piano fingers on my lap.

"I'll call Stanley Herkimer before he closes," I said. "Meanwhile, let's boil down this list of suspects."

"How about later?" he said.

$\triangledown$

Lift off

THIS IS A GREAT convention city. Around Nob Hill's four big hotels, it's hard to find a person without a name tag.

I couldn't believe the Cosmetic Surgeons of America were in town. Great timing.

Channel 8's Morning News was reporting the convention. At Moscone Center protesters were out in full force carrying "Doctor Death" effigies of Denton and Steinbrenner. And banners: STOP DEATH FOR YOUTH, FUCK TUCKS FOR BUCKS, LIPOSUCTION SUCKS, DOWN WITH LIFTS, LOOSEN UP AND LIVE, FAT IS BEAUTIFUL, FACTORY JOBS—NOT NOSE JOBS . . .

I thanked God I wasn't covering that one.

I wondered if protesters ever worked. Always the same people. Some PR guy probably started the business—"Free-lance Protesters Available. Slogans and signs to fit any occasion. You name it, we'll protest it." Franchised across the country. Sort of a benign terrorist organization.

Following the news I watched a special report by Mayor Skiathos who'd crawled out of his cave to tell us how he'd handle the $200,000,000 deficit left by his predecessor who'd been running for Governor of the state while mayor.

I switched to Channel 6 where a panel of "concerned citizens" were grilling poor Denton and Steinbrenner about the dangers of cosmetic surgery. Blowup shots of Binky, Neenie and Buffy were the backdrop of the set. A natural for Donahue, I thought.

I switched again. Channel 10's Myra Bamburger was interviewing Bellevue Paunche, the lawyer holding the Guinness world record for malpractice suits—damages awarded his clients exceeded last year's trade deficit with Japan. Paunche was about to take on the poor doctors.

I knew Paunche would get in the act, but I was hoping to keep the greedy bastard from making a case.

I'd called Stanley Herkimer twice, but no answer. Two days to analyze. I wondered how he could be that busy.

Meanwhile Rex and I were having fits narrowing down suspects when suddenly we got an idea: I'd arrange interviews with each of them, explaining that I was doing a feature on prominent social figures for the Sunday magazine section, *Reflections*, edited by our guy who thinks he's Jimmy Breslin.

I could set up some interviews that afternoon when I covered the benefit croquet match to raise money for shoring up Coit Tower, which was starting to tilt. City engineers were predicting another Pisa if something wasn't done soon.

The match was on the Marina Green and the entry fee for "Play a Day of Croquet by the Bay" was $250. Last month's *Our Crowd*—San Francisco's little society paper trying to be like the Palm Beach "shiny"—ran an article on how their little crowd had suddenly gone bananas for croquet. A new "obsession," it said, featuring a full page picture of a dumb looking guy in white knickers, leaning on his croquet mallet like he'd just bagged a Siberian tiger. (Ralph Lauren would soon have croquet outfits.)

I knew a few of our "suspects" would be playing croquet, so I'd have a chance to set up some interviews. Meanwhile I was hoping Bayview Chemists would call.

$\triangledown$

The Convict

GLANCING AT THE TABLOIDS waiting to check out my groceries, I spotted the *Intruder* "LONELY WOMAN MAR- RIES PET MALE BOA—ACLU CLAIMS HER LEGAL RIGHT" . . . "CARDINAL CORLEONI BECOMES FIRST LIVING ANGEL, HAS WING IMPLANT FROM VATI- CAN PIGEON—Furious Pope Cancels Visit to Polish Rock Concert."

Nothing unusual, but I almost wet my jeans when I read the box at the bottom of the page: "Frisco Society Scribe Denied Freedom of the Press." I turned to page 3 and there was a picture of me with prison bars superimposed over my face, captioned: "HUNTTING-MARGATE PRISON HOLDS PATTY NOTTINGHAM IN SOLITARY." The first paragraph said: "Our spies tell us Patty ('Pattie's Chatter') Nottingham knows the real story behind the bi- zarre deaths of society's Hall of Famers, but rich old socialite boss Hattie Huntting-Margate has gagged little Patty. What's the real chatter, Patty?"

The checkout girl rang up my *Intruder*, non-fat milk, caffeine-free Diet Coke, high-fiber Post Bran Flakes, Lean Cuisines, and salt-free chicken soup. Then I asked her to hold it a second, ragging everyone in back of me, while I rushed back to get a half gallon of Safeway Vodka and a carton of cigarettes. (I didn't care if the "Today" program showed my picture in sixty years.)

In the kitchen I unpacked the stuff, including Pinkus' filthy tabloid.
Then the phone rang.
Peter, my editor. It had hit the fan.
"Patty, what the hell are you up to?"
"You saw it?—"
"Everyone in the damned place has a copy, including you know who."
"It's not my fault, Peter—"
"Get your fanny down here right away. She wants to see us."
I'd be fired I knew it.

The chain smoking was really getting to her. She sounded like barbed wire had stuck in her throat.
"What's this prison crap, Patty?"
"The man's been harrassing me Mrs. Huntting-Margate." (I figured I'd lost my "H-M" privilege for the moment.)
"What man?" she rasped.
"Maximillian Pinkus. I told him on the phone I couldn't see him, so he came to my apartment but I wouldn't let him in."
"What did you tell the kike bastard?" Her left eye was squeezed shut from cigarette smoke.
"I kept saying no I can't see you and finally I told him it was against the *Journal's* policy—"
"No wonder he wrote that garbage."
I began to light one of my king-size filtered Merits.
"What's that, a Tampax? Here, have a real cigarette."
I couldn't refuse one of her Camels.
Peter came to my rescue. "Those people are relentless, H-M. They're jackals. Patty's not at fault."
I took a deep drag on my Camel and almost blacked out.

Staring me down with her laser beam right eye, H-M said, "Stay clear of those bastards, Patty. Stay out of the papers, or you'll be looking for a want-ad job in Oakland." She picked up the phone and spun around in her wheelchair. The meeting was over.

As Peter and I walked out she growled, "At least you didn't marry that boa," and went into one of her laughing/coughing fits as we shut the door.

The old bat. Some day. . . .

Space Oddity

THE CHOIR SOFTLY sang "Nobody Knows d' Trouble I've Seen" as Bombardo, king of syndicated tabloid television announced his topic for the day—"And You Think You've Got Troubles."

On stage were three sets of adult Siamese twins.

Bombardo introduced Cliff 'n Carl—wearing a cute quadruple-breasted pinstripe suit—who worked at a Baskin Robbins where they served crowds of double-scoop customers at windmill speed, always winning employee-of-the-mouth plaques, causing bitterness among two-handed employees.

Cliff, however, was in deep doodoo. Cheating on his 1040 for years, he'd been indicted by the IRS for tax fraud and faced ten years in the slammer. Brother Carl was clean as a whistle, taxwise. An unfair situation, but the IRS has its job to do. The second pair—

The phone ring pierced my sleep and I jumped a foot. Terrible dreams lately, but no surprise about this one because he was on my mind. Bombardo was in town researching cosmetic surgery scams for his next show.

It was Rex.

"Read the morning paper?"

I hadn't.

"Stanley Herkimer bought it. Janitor found him dead at his microscope—"

I was still half asleep.

"Hello . . . You there, Patty?"

"Yes, dear—"

"Your guy at Bayview Chemists. He's dead."

That snapped me out of it. "I heard y—, God, there goes my analysis."

"You can claim your stuff if you call the police right a—"

"I'm in the *Intruder*."

"What?"

"Everyone's seen it."

"What's it say?"

"Says H-M won't let me talk about the deaths. I almost got fired."

"I'll get a copy . . . but call the cops about your stuff."

I called the police and they told me to come in to sign some forms and they'd have a cop meet me at Bayview Chemists in 24 hours.

Meanwhile I could start my "suspect" interviews. At the croquet match the day before I'd already made appointments with Prudence and Mimmsy for next week. Good to see Mimmsy again. I'd worried about her.

I certainly couldn't interview H-M, but her escort Lamar Philbin would love it. I called him and he asked me to come right over.

I worried about Lamar telling H-M I was interviewing him. I thought I'd better explain it was confidential and that I planned to surprise her with my article.

The Universe of Lamar design studio occupied the top floor of an old industrial building on upper Market Street. He'd decorated it in a sort of Star Trek motif, like the inside of the Enterprise. His staff, all males, sort of, wore "space" outfits. His garments cutters had false ears ala Spock. A real nuthouse, and this was no dream.

Lamar Philbin, in a gold lamé jump suit and suede elf slippers, beamed me into an office reminiscent of an astronaut testing chamber. On its curved walls were gown designs and photographs of what were probably his stable of boyfriends—all dressed in leotards with Baryshnikov crotch lumps.

We sat in gold beanbag chairs.

"I've created an atmosphere for far out thinking," he said, looking down at his crotch. "My designs look beyond."

Lamar's nose was red and I don't think he had a cold. His voice squeaked like Truman Capote's.

"Ever designed anything traditional, Mr. Philbin?"

"Yes, for a slut in New York who made drecky things for Montgomery Ward. My first job . . . I try to forget it." He stared at me with soft boiled, red-veined eyes. "And call me Lamar. I'm dropping the 'Philbin'."

He pointed to a sketch of one of his creations. It looked like a hoola hoop with blue mosquito netting.

"See that," he said. "The outer ring is her statement of challenge. Saturn's her future. The netting's her universe."

Jesus.

He pointed to another sketch with his white wormy fingers.

"My latest. The idea beamed down to me on my balcony one night."

Right after a line or two, I thought.

The model, completely wrapped in silver wire, looked like a human electric coil.

"I call it 'Galactic Woman, 3000'. I'll sell only one of these."

Lots of luck.

"You've just seen my profoundest fashion statements."

I could see Lamar doing a fashion show to Toakhime's music.

Now for some Q and A for my so-called feature article,

with questions slipped in to help my investigation.

"Have you designed gowns for our social set, Mr. Ph—, Lamar?"

"Not yet, and I'm just furious."

Lamar's face looked like a bar of Dove soap with inflamed nostrils.

"Those trollops feel safe with drones like de Larenta and Adolfo."

"Have patience, Lamar." I said, smiling and looking at the things on his desk for clues.

"They'd best hurry. The Universe shrinks as we speak."

"Your designs *are* a bit dramatic, Lamar."

"Fools said that about the hydrogen bomb."

We talked more about his insane designs. Then I slid into some social chatter hoping he wouldn't see through my hoax.

"Did you know Binky, Neenie and Buffy?"

"H-M introduced me," he said, starting to squirm in his chair.

"Why do you think they died? They were so healthy and happ—"

"It was their time," he said, not seeming to give a damn.

"Where's your photographer?"

I lied, promising that Eddie would see him next week to take photographs for the article.

"Known H-M long?"

"Since man's Universe called her husband two years ago." He looked up through the ceiling.

I wasn't surprised he called it *man's* Universe. "So nice of you to escort H-M," I said. "Poor dear's hip won't heal."

"She needs me," he said, excusing himself to go to his private john, returning happier than when he left.

"Now, where were we?" he said, arranging himself in the beanbag chair. "Oh, yes, poor old H-M. She's on her way too, but we had fun that night."

"You sat at their tables (I assumed he'd been at Binky's

table too.) Did they look sick?"

"Looked fine to me . . . except for their dreadful gowns."

Since the stare he'd given me during his Montgomery Ward story, he'd avoided eye contact and kept looking down at his lap as I conversed with his bleached crew cut.

Then he said, "I'd left before they were called."

"Where'd they go?"

Crossing his delicate gold lamé legs, he said, "To the Universe."

The guy was nutty enough to be the phantom killer.

"Think they could have eaten or drunk something that caused the universe to call them?"

"It was their time, Patty, and I'm sick of talking about it."

Then he jumped up and squeaked, "I must join my crew."

Like an arthritic I struggled out of my gold beanbag.

"I'll be expecting your photographer," he said, leaving me without a goodbye.

I yelled a thank you and beamed myself out.

I wondered if he was just an escort for H-M. Perhaps they were working together.

No matter what, Lamar Philbin was a suspect.

At home my answering machine said I should call Sergeant Geary at police headquarters. I called and four turnovers later Geary answered and told me to meet him at Bayview Chemists tomorrow at 9:00 A.M.

Batter Up

GEARY, A CUTE IRISH-FACED cop (they look so young) was waiting outside the old building on Howard Street.

Herkimer's Transylvania lab had been cleaned up. One big table was filled with hundreds of beakers, bottles, test tubes and glass saucers—some empty, some with stuff in them.

I pointed to my little bottle and Geary handed it to me.

"Yours ma'am?"

"Yes officer."

"Have an anxiety problem ma'am?"

I wondered what was he talking about.

"My wife's a nervous wreck too. I'm broke buying Valium."

I explained the Valium bottle and he understood. I opened it. Empty.

My writing professor always said, "build conflict; make it tough on the protagonist." I thought if this built anymore I'd go crazy. I was screwed if the weapon was gone . . . if it *was* the weapon, and I thought it was. The "smoking gun," as they say in Washington. The police reported Herkimer died of old age, but I wondered if he'd been quietly knocked off by someone who was onto my investigation.

Then I saw a smaller table with stacks of little pieces of glass.

"May I check these, officer?"

"The slides? G'right ahead ma'am."

I found two slides taped together with a squashed pale yellow glob between them—like a little glass sandwich.

"Pretty sure this is it, Officer Geary. Make I take this and my Valium bottle?"

"Just sign this form, ma'am."

I put the little glass sandwich inside the Valium bottle, thanked Geary and left.

At home I put it back in the freezer behind my sugar-free fudgsicles, thinking about asking Marvin for another chemist.

Too early to call Rex so I got ready for the luncheon benefit sponsored by "Friends of the Battered"—a sort of "summit" for all "battered" groups—wives, mistresses, kids, husbands, mother-in-laws.

I stopped by the paper first to read my galley on tomorrow's column—"Polo sans Ponies, the New Obsession." Peter had scratched out my lead in—"Balls out for Croquet"—and written something cute in the margin. We kidded around a lot.

While I was reading, Peter rushed up to my desk and asked what the hell I was doing interviewing Lamar Philbin.

The little weirdo had already told H-M, even after I'd asked him to keep it confidential.

"My article was to be a surprise, Peter," I said, hating to lie. "I'd planned to show you the draft. A little supplement for my 'such a fucking bore' column, as you call it." It embarrassed me to say the "F" word and Peter knew it.

"Sorry Patty, but she went bananas. Wanted me to fire you."

"What can I say?" I said.

"No more fooling around, that's what you can say."

"I'll go sit in the corner."

He leaned over and kissed my cheek. Peter's a dear.

The "Friends of the Battered" luncheon was in the upstairs of John's Grill where whatshisname wrote *The Mal-*

tese Falcon. Rather small crowd but I suppose most of the invited guests were still recovering in the hospital.

Already at the microphone, Supervisor Sal Mancotti had begun raving about a new study to get at the "root cause of battering."

The usual patrons and lump of climbers were there, including Sophie Jacobs who had a new lift—she now looked like Madam Chiang Kai Shek.

Mancotti droned on, digressing the way he does, preaching about the scourge of cosmetic malpractice, asking for money to print photographs of Denton's and Steinbrenner's patients on non-fat milk cartons. I hadn't the slightest idea why.

H-M wasn't at the Battered lunch. Just the main events for her.

During quiche and salad, former battered husband Clay Marlboro, a delicate little man, spoke of his trauma and introduced his smiling wife who was built like William Perry of the Chicago Bears. Marlboro, still a little wobbly, then plugged his book, *Stand on Your Own Two Feet.*

As I left, the lump followed me downstairs smiling and telling me how nice it was to see me again. You can recognize climbers by their Vuitton bags. Old money and society don't need status symbols.

Thankful to be out of there, I headed for the office to write my column and maybe call Marvin.

In my mailbox that evening were bills, junk mail and a yellow slip saying I had a registered letter at the Post Office. The originating zip code on the slip was 10022—Manhattan.

⟡

Architectural Digest

WALKING DOWN THE HALL to my office the next day I passed our movie critic Gerald Boswell and asked if he'd seen any good movies lately, prompting him to ask if I'd been to any good parties lately.

Except for Boswell who reads only his own galleys, everyone had read the *Intruder*. I was sick to death of telling them it was a lie.

Boswell recognized me by my voice. Film critics have weak eyes because they watch movies morning, noon and night, and never see daylight. Actually, Boswell hates movies—beneath his sense of art, so he pans them all. Claims he's really a playwright, but he's never sold a word.

Nobody cares about movie reviews anyway except the Hollywood crowd. Most people who go to films don't read newspapers. They watch the hot stuff critics on television—the fat guy . . . and the bald guy who never lets you forget he went to Yale. They're pretty easy on new movies. Why should they kill the goose?

But enough about Boswell's profession which is almost as useless as mine. I had to get my "Friends of the Battered" copy approved.

After Peter okayed my column, he said, "Can you get some help for battered editors?" Peter also edits the *Journal's* entire entertainment section, an enormous responsibility. *Applause* is the best read section of the paper.

"How's the old battle ax?" I asked.

"Fighting with Junior again."

Running the *Journal* wasn't a bowl of cherries for Rudolph Huntting-Margate, Junior, with Mama still owning more stock than he did. And it must have driven the old grandame nuts that Junior was leaning more and more to the left.

I'd often thought because they get such crappy salaries from their billionaire owners, newspaper writers tend to be liberal, which was maybe rubbing off on Junior. And which was probably why H-M was smoking so many Camels.

I doubted Dudley Crenshaw or the other husbands would give me time for interviews, but I knew Dudley's girlfriend Shotsie would love it. I figured I could pick up a clue or two from her.

Shotsie Fenner, divorced more than Liz Taylor, loved the whirl. Shotsie was old money San Francisco, but had been drummed out of the Register ten years ago for marrying her Porsche mechanic. That hadn't held her down though; her old friends still loved Shotsie and she was involved in most all the boring events I covered.

She agreed to see me at 11 A.M. at her Clay/Jones apartment.

A tiny Asian maid answered the door and directed me into the living room where Shotsie, sprawled across a chinoiserie-covered love seat, smiled at me with all her thirty-two capped teeth. She had on a to-die-over Armani at-home of pale orange and yellow, and the place looked like *Architectural Digest*.

"Come sit. So nice to see you, Patty *deah*."

Another Westerner with a British accent.

She pointed to the love seat across from her and I sat down. Between our love seats was an antique Chinese black lacquer coffee table worth more than my car, clothes and all the furniture in my dumpy little apartment.

"Drink? White wine? Bloody?" she asked, narrowing to twenty-four teeth. She was long, scrawny, and aging, but still attractive, like a well maintained vintage car. Blond hair in a sort of King Tut style. About fifty. Seemed everyone I knew was about fifty . . . or eighteen and coming out.

I thanked her for the offer, but said I was working and a cup of coffee would be fine.

"Saw your cute picture in that awful rag," she said. "My maid brought it home."

No one in this crowd read the tabloids. Only their maids.

I explained the Pinkus visit and how H-M was furious with me.

"So sorry for you deah, but she'll get over it."

The tiny maid brought my black coffee and Shotsie's bloody mary with a foot long celery stalk sticking out of it. Shotsie's crowd celebrated late mass for bloody mary every morning at 11, after which the body of Christ was served in the form of eggs benedict.

I told her I'd been working on an article featuring our city's "style setters and fun lovers."

She smiled—back to thirty-two teeth—and said she'd be delighted to be in the article.

"I saw you with Dudley Crenshaw at the Deb Ball," I said.

"We sat at Buffy's table, poor deah." Shotsie'd stopped smiling and I could finally see her face.

Think it was really a stroke?" I asked.

"So the doctor said, God knows, she was just scads of fun that night. Poor deah. Must have happened after we all left the table."

That's what Lamar had said to me previously.

She took a big gulp of bloody mary, adroitly dodging the celery. Her face was Palm Desert tan, and when she stopped smiling the cracks turned white.

"After dinner we were drinking bubbly and dancing," she said. "Dear little Buffy was tres gay . . . oops, wrong word . . . so delighted with her little parade of Debs."

Shotsie loved talking about parties, so I kept her rolling. I told her I'd seen Lamar Philbin.

"I could never wear Lamar's things," she said.

"Too far out?"

"An apt description, deah." She smiled again—twenty-four teeth. "Lamar sat next to Buffy. Kissed her a—pampered her all night. Filled her wine glass after every sip she took. Pesty little devil. Plucked a flower off the centerpiece and pinned it on her gown. Right under her little nose. Things like that."

I jotted that down in my notebook, wondering if Lamar dropped the little thing in Buffy's glass while he was doing all that pampering. Or was Shotsie, being guilty herself, suggesting Lamar was the murderer?

She continued. "Prudence Landsdale-Chase sat on Lamar's right. Pru, of course, has taken a new name. Married that nice black doctor. Can't ever remember his name—sounds like that basketball chap in Hollywood."

Boolibar Jabbar-Lamumba," I said.

"Right. I sat next to him. Charming. And big, I must say." Her mouth opened wide and her eyes rolled.

Boolie was one man Shotsie hadn't tried yet.

"I don't see why people fussed about their marriage so," she said. "The whole world will be all cafe au lait soon anyway."

She rang for the maid, continuing her one way conversation. "He talked about Chad," she said. "Thought it was a friend of his at first. Never heard of the bloody place. Doctor Jabbar's doing something for a medical clinic there—a little project about fertility or longer life . . . I forget. Doesn't seem they need more fertility in Africa, if you know what I mean."

"Prudence seems happy," I said, barely able to get in a word.

"Prudence is in love. Simply adores the man. And so grateful to her friends for accepting him, if you know what I mean. His family owns miles of cotton plantations. One of the richest families in North Africa."

Better than being from Oakland, I thought.

Then she winked. "Think they have white folks pickin' their cotton?"

She thought that was pretty funny and almost poked her eye with the celery stalk.

"H-M was there. A good soldier," I said, keeping Shotsie rolling along.

"Dear old H-M in that dreadful wheelchair. Poor thing sat between Rod and Dud. Stupid Dudley asked her to dance."

Hmm, I thought. How come she remembered precisely where everyone sat? That party was a while ago.

The maid brought out another bloody mary and more hot coffee.

We discussed Shotsie's social life, clothes, likes, dislikes, her interior designer, her jewelry. A regular Barbara Walters number. Her third "bloody" and I couldn't shut her up. I felt she was maybe being a little too cooperative.

By 1 P.M. I'd talked my way out of her apartment. No lunch yet and I was starved.

I couldn't wait to talk over my notes with Rex. But first I'd get some lunch and then walk to Marvin's. No, I'd call Marvin.

"Marvin? Patty Nottingham."

"Hi Patty. Cute picture of you in the *Intruder*?"

"I'll tell you about it when I see you, Marvin. I'm calling to tell you Mr. Herkimer died in the middle of my chemical analysis."

"I heard. And only eighty-four. Probably needed more fiber."

"I found my stuff in his lab, Marvin. Between two slides."

"Lucky you found it. He was a slob."

"Know another chemist?"

"Jack London Chemists in Oakland."

Oakland, dear God.

"Name's Herman Kleindienst."

"You'll call for me?"

"I think he'll remember me. In my class at pharmacy school."

"Thanks, Marvin."

"Clever the way they drew the jail bars in front of you."

"Don't forget to call Kleindienst, Marv."

"Don't worry," he said. I heard his little doorbell tinkle as he said goodbye.

▽

Don't Give me Flowers

I CALLED JACK LONDON Chemists and Herman Kleindienst answered—another one man operation. We made a date for eleven the next morning.

Then I called Rex who'd left a message on my machine saying "Where the hell are you?"

Rex came over and we talked about Lamar Philbin and Shotsie Fenner.

"First of all," I said. "Lamar's crazy. Even without snorting he'd be nuts."

"Think he did it?"

"Could be. He despises my rich ladies."

"They don't buy his gowns?"

"God no, and I wonder who would. The designs are worse than he is."

"And he dates that old Huntting-Margate?"

"She's his key to society."

"I've got it," Rex said, showing a little excitement. For Rex anyway. "They're both pissed. The old dame hasn't had a man in years like her pretty friends have, and now she's stuck in a wheelchair and can't even dance. And Lamar's going broke because those broads don't buy his crazy dresses. There've been murders committed for less."

"A regular *Columbo*," I said. "So you're saying their

82

motives are: She can't dance and he can't sell any dresses?"

"That's it," Rex said, looking triumphant.

"What a world." I kissed his cheek, smooth as a baby's because of the new Norelco Cordless 900 I'd bought him. Then I thought of something. "Remember when you mentioned flowers . . . about stamens and pistils?"

"I hated that course in high school—"

"Shotsie said Lamar was overattentive toward Buffy. Filling her wine glass after every sip, dancing with her almost every number, and get this—he picked a flower from the centerpiece and pinned it to the top of Buffy's dress."

"Fashion guys always have pins," Rex said.

"Don't you get it, Rex dear? The flower could have been toxic."

"Listen to the chemist. What kind of flower?"

"I'll try to find out from Buffy's decorating committee."

"Did this Shotsie say Lamar pinned flowers on Binky and Neenie?"

"Shotsie wasn't at their tables. Remember?"

"We should find out if he did."

"I'll work on it."

I detailed my Shotsie interview to Rex. Explained how I thought she could be a suspect, the way she seemed to overemphasize Lamar's activities and how she'd remembered precisely where each of them sat that night.

He took my hand and said, "You never know. In the movies people least suspected are the murderers and we don't have a butler . . . But enough sleuthing."

He leaned over and kissed me and in a few minutes we were going at it right there on my white velveteen couch.

We showered—I had to be the cleanest person at the *Journal*. But I was proud of my new body; the flab was almost gone. Rex didn't seem to care though. "You're a wonderful human being, Patty," he kept saying as we washed each other.

"Wise ass," I said, smiling and stretching his long member.

"More," he said, smiling in his dirty way.

I let it snap back and he hugged me.

I began dressing for the office and Rex put on his maroon and white Nike warmup suit.

Going out the door, he said, "Let me know what the Jack London guy finds. Maybe it's a poison pistil."

I laughed and threw him a kiss. My mouth was too sore for a real one.

▽

Hoboken by the Bay

DRESSING FOR MY TRIP to Jack London Chemists, I watched Bombardo on Channel 10 doing his "Skin Merchants of Tragedy."

Four victims—all women—sat on the stage. Bombardo's investigative staff had dug up the worst. One's ears had sprouted long white hair, and her eyes were held open with duct tape. The second one's nose was gone except for its shotgun barrel nostrils. The third's eyeballs were on permanent high beam—couldn't shut or blink her eyes, requiring her to sleep in a gallows hood. And the fourth looked like a before-and-after nosedrop commercial —on one side of her face the mouth drooped, the closed eye dripped tears and the nostril kept running . . . the other side had a youthful smile, clear nostril and a happy bright eye. Looked like her doctor'd been called to the phone in the middle of the operation.

The victims' two doctors were in silhouette behind a curtain and two guests neurosurgeons sat alongside the victims.

The television audience looked like standbys at a bus station.

Bombardo introduced the "victims" and doctors, referring to the silhouettes as Doctors X and Y.

He touched on the "alleged" cosmetic fatalities of Binky, Neenie and Buffy, omitting their names and their doctors,

Denton and Steinbrenner, probably because he worried about law suits.

I'd heard Denton and Steinbrenner had closed their practices and gone fishing.

That show would be the beginning of the end of "lift" and "lipo." Next would be *Donahue, Oprah, Sixty Minutes*, and all the tabloid television programs.

My big chance had arrived. I'd discover the murderer, and the Association of Cosmetic Surgeons would be more than grateful. And as Rex said, I'd be famous. Best of all—no more silly column to write. No more Huntting-Margate. And maybe the cops would listen to me next time.

"Have you suffered from your obvious disfigurement, Mrs. Kirkman?"

"Except for looshing my hushband and friendsh, I guessh I'm O.K. Can't get a job, but at leasht I can watsch TV."

The audience applauded.

"Have you sued Doctor X, Mrs. Kirkman?"

As if Bombardo didn't know.

"Oh yesh," she said.

"Did the jury award damages for your hideous looking nose bob, Mrs. Kirkman?"

"A two year trial, shir, but I finally won the cashe."

"Cash?"

"No, cashe . . . C-A-SH-E."

"How much, Mrs. Kirkman?"

"Shixsh hundred thousand—"

"With all that money, Mrs. Kirkman, why not have your nose fixed?"

"After the lawyersh were through I jusht had enough to buy Kleenexsh."

Bombardo, cordless mike in hand, walked among the biddies in the audience to get comments.

I couldn't stand it any longer and shut it off.

Another old industrial building. In the heart of Oakland's

dock area where ships were unloading boxes of Toyotas and Nissans. Busier than our poor docks.

I walked up one long flight of stairs and found the entrance. A big fat guy with red-grey hair introduced himself as Herman Kleindienst and led me to his work table. It was a dump but neater than Herkimer's.

I took the Valium bottle out of my purse and removed the slides with the stuff in between and gave it to him.

"Stanley must've had it under his microscope already, Ma'am. Good thing he didn't drop it in his catalytic centrifuge. You'd never have found it."

I didn't ask about the centrifuge business.

"Too bad about Stanley. Good chemist."

"Sweet old man," I said.

"You know what they say, Ma'am . . . old chemists never die, they just lose their pestles." With that he laughed so hard his cigar dropped from his gross brown teeth.

I smiled not to hurt his feelings, and then asked when he'd finish analyzing my stuff.

"Late today. Hundred bucks."

Overhead's cheaper in Oakland. Rex calls it the Hoboken of the West.

"Wonderful," I said.

"Unless it's a complex compound that needs special catalysts or special testing equipment."

I figured with my luck it would be something no chemist had ever come across.

He wrote my order and home phone on a billing pad Bob Cratchet might have used in A Christmas Carol, then walked me to his mottled glass Sam Spade door and out into the hall.

"I'll be at that number after five this evening," I said. "And tomorrow morning 'til 10:30 . . . or leave a message on my machine. Thanks Mr. Kliendienst."

$\triangledown$

The Botanist

WE DECIDED TO RESEARCH flowers to see if any were poisonous. The only dangerous plants I knew were cactus and that fly-eating thing. Rex had gone to the library and xeroxed pages on "Flowers" from the *FINNI-GANGR* Funk & Wagnall.

After I kissed Rex hello I said "hello birdie," in a high voice to Gershwin, his canary. Gershwin sang a lot and if he wasn't singing, Rex played Gershwin's tapes. The canary Gershwin, not George. Fascinated by the canary's numerous singing patterns Rex kept a little tape recorder next to his cage and turned it on when he left the apartment, believing Gershwin was too shy to sing all his numbers, particularly his obscure ones, with people around. Rex claimed his bird's repertoire was better than that of most rock singers and he loved the cheerful ambiance. I agreed with him but when both the canary and the tape were going at the same time it was a little too much.

Gershwin lived on top of the old studio piano Rex had bought from a grammar school that closed in the Mission district. Except when Rex played, the keys usually had a sprinkling of birdseed on them. Sometimes a few feathers. So I was making a thing out of my old red blouse to put around the bottom of the cage.

The endless NFL playoffs were dominating Rex's weekends, but the one-sided Atlanta-Washington game that day didn't interest him that much. We usually had a quick roll in the sheets at halftime which I didn't enjoy that much, but I did love Rex. If he wanted sex, I gave it to him—like the editor of *Cosmo* said. I never had that trouble with Charlie Nottingham, so I was thankful for Rex's activity.

On a coffee table made from an old bass drum he had the xeroxed pages and began reading the sentences he'd highlighted in yellow: "It says here: 'the flower is the reproductive organ of the angio-sperm plant that produces fruit containing seeds'."

The football game was on but no sound. Second quarter—28 zip. Atlanta led, with four minutes 'til halftime. I figured four football minutes would take twenty.

" 'The floral axis or receptacle—' " Rex looked up from the book and smiled—"That's the pretty flower part, 'bears one to four specialized appendages, arranged in whorls. The outermost whorl, the calyx, consists of sepals. The next whorl is the corolla (petals) bearing nectar-producing glands that attract pollinators'."

His mouth was cute when he said "whorl."

" 'The next whorl, the androecium—' "

He had trouble with that one.

" 'consists of a number of stamens which produce pollen for reproduction in anthers.' "

"Never knew flowers had so much fun," I said.

His hand dropped to my lap.

" 'The innermost or highest whorl called the gyno . . . gynoecium, consists of carpels frequently confused with the pistil.' "

I squeezed his hand.

" 'Each carpel has one placenta with connecting ovules.' "

Reminded me, I needed to see my gynecologist.

" 'The calyx and corolla are collectively called the perianth.' "

"I'll remember that, dear, if you ever bring me a bouquet."
He kissed my ear.

" 'It is a perfect flower if all reproductive organs are present. If only pistils are present the flower is said to be "pistillate." With stamens only, "staminate." Typical flowers are bisexual.' "

"Like Cary Grant," I said.

" 'When staminate and pistillate occur in one plant it is said to be mono . . . monoecious; when they occur on different plants, dioecious.' "

"Like on Castro Street."

Even before the announcer came on with scores and highlights, Rex grabbed my hand and said, "Let's give it a whorl."

Sometimes he reaches too far for a gag, but if you're in love, it's better to go along than to ridicule. Particularly when you're not yet married.

Back on the couch I said, "Haven't heard anything bad yet."

"Listen to this," Rex said, pointing to "FRAGRANCE."
"Fragrance is caused by minute quantities of volatile oils formed by the alteration of essential oils in petals—"

"So?"

" 'Some flowers give off evil odors'."

"Hmm."

" 'Such flowers', it says, 'are called carrion flowers and usually smell like rotting flesh'."

"What else does it say?"

"Then it says, 'see HORTICULTURE or BOTANY'."

"Is that all you have?"

"Sorry."

"Terrific."

$\triangledown$

Such a Mess

THE OZONE SCARE SOUNDS worse than smog. At least you can spot smog. You can't even see ozone and without it we'll all melt.

That evening I covered a cocktail party staged by "Friends of the Ozone."

Hundred bucks a head for white wine, toothpick-skewered meatballs, a handshake from Fannie Doerflinger and a speech by Berkeley's Professor of Environmental Studies, Doctor Harkness Kram. Keynote speaker was Supervisor Sal Mancotti.

We were outside Sophie Jacob's penthouse on her thousand-foot terrace underneath the depleting ozone. Sophie's Madam Chiang Kai Shek look had sagged a bit and she was having difficulty smiling. She needed a new tuck, but Dr. Denton was in hiding.

Mancotti suggesting banning all aerosol cans of whipped cream, and Fannie Doerflinger asked for money (Fannie was probably stashing away more money for herself than she was for whales, libraries and the ozone). Doctor Kram told us we'd all be toasted marshmallow with cancer by the year 2,000.

Before leaving I made notes on who would be bold-faced. Then I walked to the elevator, wading through the climbers who were telling me how nice it was to see me.

When I opened my front door a sick feeling hit me. Just like in a murder mystery, my apartment had been ransacked. My little desk drawers had been emptied and my junk was all over the floor. In the kitchen the refrigerator was open and my leftover Weight Watchers lasagna had been knocked into the sugar-free lime Jello. In the bedroom clothes were strewn all over.

A typed note stuck up from the roller in my new Mitsubishi electric typewriter:

KEE P YOUR LITTLE N OSE OUT O F THINGS OR YO UR ASHES WILL BE WITH TH E OTHER LIT TLE BITCHES.

I liked the part about the little nose, but I was scared to death and wanted to call the police. Then I decided I wanted to get this bastard myself.

I tore over to the Mark Hopkins to talk to Rex. He saw me and began playing "What's New?".

I walked to the piano and showed him the note. He stopped playing and said I should move in with him for a few days and get a burglar alarm system installed in my place. Meanwhile I should call the police, he said. I said screw the police.

"Sorry I suggested you investigate," Rex said. "I'm worried, Patty."

I looked into his eyes and said, "I'd rather die than write that boring column the rest of my life."

"Did they get the stuff?"

"I told you. Kleindienst has it."

"Who's Kleindienst?"

"Jack London Chemists."

"Great."

"They ruined my lime Jello."

"You're lucky that's all, and howdyknow it's a 'they'?"

"Cause we don't know it's a she or a he."

"Gotta get back to the work, sweetheart. Go to my place and stay there. If a car tries to run you down on the sidewalk, step into a store front or someone's walkway."

He really did care about me.

▽

Flower Alert

I'D STAYED IN REX'S apartment that night, and before I went to work the next morning I went home to change for the office and clean up the mess. Being daytime, I wasn't as scared walking in, but I knocked loudly and waited a few minutes before unlocking the door.

At work I finished my column and then went to the *Journal's* library to research poisonous flowers and plants.

When I returned to Rex's apartment that evening, he was already dressing for his cocktail piano session.

"Be out soon as I'm dressed," he yelled from the bedroom.

When he walked into the living room in his black tie, I had a little seizure. So handsome and sexy, I wanted him right there on the couch, but I restrained myself. The nuns at Dominican High had taught me that.

"Got time to talk flowers?"

"Sorry I didn't get you any—"

"You never do."

He smiled. "I know, you mean poison pistils and stuff. Good idea."

"I checked out 'Plants, poison' in the library."

"Funk and Wagnall?"

"I think so."

"Good girl," he said, sitting next to me on the couch. "I

couldn't live without Funk and Wagnall when I was in school."

"It shocked me," I said. "So many innocent, pretty plants contain poison. Practically every drug is made from plant stuff, and I'm not talking about pot and cocaine."

"Poison Ivy's a bitch."

"No, dear. I mean real poison. These plants are all around us."

"But what about *flowers*?"

"All plants have some sort of flower. The beautiful cherry blossom, for instance. Know where cyanide comes from?"

"Not *cherries* for chrissake."

"Yes."

"And you're eating cherries jubilee all the time."

"Not those cherries, dear. Wild cherries. Cyanide comes from the glycoside in the plant part."

"Good dessert for my ex-wife—Wild Cherries Glycoside."

"Stop it, Rex. I'm serious."

"So am I."

"The pretty oleander plant is deadly, for instance."

"Christ. California'll be wiped out. They're all over the place."

"You'd have to swallow a load of them, dear. The leaves I think. The type of poison in plants attacks the nervous system, like the alkaloids in hemlock."

"And that Lamar character was screwing around with the flowers in the centerpiece."

"I can't see how pinning a little flower on someone would kill them."

"Maybe that little stick's concentrated plants and flowers, like they make instant coffee."

"And maybe Lamar dropped the stuff in the ladies' champagne glasses when they weren't looking, when he was fooling around giving them flowers and pouring their wine."

"Like Shotsie said."

$\triangledown$

Fun in the Lab

LONELY DAYS WERE AHEAD. Rex flew to New York to deal with this ex-wife who'd been harrassing him about alimony payments. With his charm I figured he'd work it out, but naturally I was worried about her trying to get him back. In the sack for a few nights if nothing else. One day without sex made Rex crabby.

But those were mean thoughts. I loved Rex and wanted to be with him forever, even though I knew an aging cocktail pianist had no great future—arthritis of the fingers and goodbye Cole Porter. I didn't push him though; men hate that. I knew it and so did the editor of *Cosmo*.

Rex had ability, but he thought he was over the hill. Being fired from *KHIP* had hurt and he'd sort of given up.

The Bohemian Club asked him to join for his piano talents and I thought he could have made lots of business contacts there, but he said peeing on redwood trees wasn't his thing.

I wondered did he love me or was I just a convenience. With all the women around he could certainly have found a young bomber sexier than I was. Not that I was all that unattractive. I looked in my bathroom mirror that morning and saw I was nice and trim. My exercycle and piano player kept me toned (tone was the new thing). But I worried about my "big beautiful knockers" as Rex called them. I was a bit large for my 5 foot 2, 105 pound body and in a few years they could turn into baguettes like on the women in *National Geographic*. But I expected Dr. Denton to return before then.

The phone rang and I hoped it was Kleindienst. I'd expected his call yesterday.

"Miss Nottingham?"

"Yes."

"Kleindienst at Jack London. It'll take another day or two."

"Oh dear—"

"That stuff doesn't react to my tests."

I knew it couldn't be something simple.

"How much more?" I asked.

"Another hundred should do it."

"Go ahead." I needed that hundred for my overdue Datsun payment. "You'll call me?"

"Right, lady."

"Before you go, Mr. Kleindienst, do you know of any poisonous flowers?"

"Any what?"

"Flowers, like in bouquet."

"Oh, *flowers*, thoughtcha said *showers*. I heard of a few lady, but I forget. Flowers aren't my thing."

"Thanks, don't forget to call."

"Right."

I hung up, hoping Rex would be home before the Kleindienst report.

Meanwhile I got ready for my 11 A.M. interview with Prudence Jabbar-Lamumba.

A cute, dimpled blond maid opened the heavy black enameled door and said "good morning" in a thick Scandinavian accent. From the large entry hall I could see Prudence standing in her solarium just off the huge, high-ceilinged living room.

Miss Scandinavia led me back to Prudence who said, "How nice to see you, Patty deah." No smile.

The room had a dynamite view of the Golden Gate. We rarely say "bridge."

"You look divine, Prudence." As low on the pole as society writers are at their newspapers, they're thick as thieves with the city's social set. First name basis always. After all society writers are their press agents.

I had the feeling she didn't find it "so nice to see me." Probably a bit early in her day. Or she had a hangover.

I reminded her about my "trend setters" article and how I wanted to feature her "stunning" fashion and interior design.

"Why me?" she snapped. Her terse reaction surprised me. Prudence had always been a fashion leader and mainstay of the social columns.

"Don't be modest, Prudence." I switched on my interviewer smile.

Trying to warm up, she asked how she could help.

"This *divine* solarium. Only you could create such utter charm." That revved her up.

"Thank you, dear."

She gestured toward two leopard skin wing-back chairs, and we sat down. Next to our chairs were end tables made of elephants' feet with huge yellowed toenails.

"Booly's parents gave us these as wedding presents. They're such dears."

She'd perked up a bit. Had I cut through her cool mood? I took out my reporter's notebook.

"I'd love to meet the doctor," I said.

"He's puttering in his little la*bor*atory."

Prudence exuded noble beauty. She reminded me of the duchess with the swept back blond hair at Wimbledon who hands the platters to Navritalova.

"Seems strange without Buffy, Neenie and Binky," I said.

"I begged them to stop draining their little bodies and

stretching their pretty skin," she said, lighting a low-every-thing *Merit* cigarette.

She was blaming Denton and Steinbrenner.

"You were with the ladies all three evenings. Must've been shocking."

"Dreadful," she said. "We found out later. Booly and I'd left before they'd—"

They all said that. Were they lying? Was there someone not at their table who did it? Another guest? . . . It could have been anyone . . . A waiter? . . . That gave me an idea . . . But why had I ever started this?'

"Think they could have been murdered?" I said, deciding to get right to it.

Prudence's noble mouth burst open like Al Jolson singing "Mammy," exposing her gold molars. "How can you think of such a dreadful thing?" she said.

"I'm sorr—"

"Everyone adored those women. They never hurt anyone in their lives."

11:10: Already late for mass. The maid came in and took Pru's order for a bloody mary and mine for black coffee.

"Patty, deah, may we get on with what you came here for?"

We talked fashion. Her favorite designers. What she thought the trends were. I said I'd love to photograph her in one of her favorites. She loved that.

Miss Scandinavia brought in my coffee and the bloody with a celery stalk taller than Shotsie's. Pru's face lit up as she took her drink from the tray.

"You're always so chic, Prudence—"

"You're so kind, deah."

"What do you think of Lamar Philbin's designs?"

"Divine for Halloween parties." She chuckled at her little dig, then drained half her bloody mary, expertly dodging the celery stalk.

I chuckled, acknowledging her chuckle.

"Lamar sat at your table those three evenings, didn't h—?"

"Are we getting back to *that*, Patty? Pleeeze . . ."

"No one's buying his gowns," I said. "He's furious."

"Are you suggesting . . . ?" she said with a little grin.

"Just a thought. He is a little weird."

We slid into interior design. I asked who decorated her apartment and she said Booly and she had. I looked pleasantly surprised.

The living room was definitely *Architectural Digest*, but with African accents. She called it a "touch of Safari." Two footstools of zebra skin. A tribal shield and a witch doctor mask sharing a wall with Manet and Pisarro. A white rhino head over the fireplace. The Steinway draped with cheetah skin. A few shrunken heads in with the Boehm bird collection.

"Limited eclectic" she said.

Dr. Boolibar Jabbar-Lamumba suddenly appeared.

"Excuse my appearance," he said. "I did not know we were honored with a beautiful guest." He bowed and kissed my hand. I could see why Pru went for this hunk. Charming and handsome, a young Belafonte with a French accent. Only darker.

"Just taking a breather. I am in the midst of an expcriment."

He wore a long white lab coat sprinkled with little brown blood stains and tiny spots of various colors.

"Patty just adores our apartment, deah."

"A distinct pleasure having you Madam Nottingham. If you have time, please come see my laboratory. It is a far cry from my facility in Chad, but it is adequate for continuing at least some of my projects. How do you say, better than a stick in your nose."

"I don't believe Patty will have time, my love," said Prudence.

I was dying to see his lab.

The maid delivered the second bloody mary. I'd declined more coffee. I was getting hungry, but didn't expect lunch from Prudence.

"What's your experiment, Dr. Jabbar?" I said, getting up and walking around the solarium admiring the flowers.

"Just call me 'Booly', Madam Nottingham." He smiled. Perfect white teeth contrasted with his dark face. Gorgeous. Turned me on a bit.

I smiled back. "Just call me Patty."

Prudence said, "Patty and I are in the middle of something, Booly, deah."

She didn't want me to see his lab.

"We're about through, Prudence," I said, looking at Booly.

"Come on then," he said, taking my arm.

"Please Booly," Prudence shouted as we walked away. "don't show her that dreadful mess."

"But why not?" Booly shouted back, smiling exuberantly as we walked into the large white kitchen where the maid was mixing another bloody for Prudence.

We went though the kitchen to a door with a red light blinking over it. Booly unlocked it.

The noise was deafening. We walked past a long lab table full of paraphernalia—bunsen burners, test tubes, blenders and lots of other things. A big jar of cloudy liquid containing a bunch of gross, brown fleshy bags sat on one end of the table and on the other end was a glass aquarium-like box with a bunch of intertwined snakes. All over the room were cages—bouncing up and down, swaying form side to side— big cages containing pairs of monkeys and rows of little cages with pairs of mice, rats, gerbils and hamsters.

Except for the icky, blue-back snakes which did nothing but weave around, all the animals were humping each other like crazy. Tiny black and white mice squealed with joy, straddling their mates. And the monkeys—we all know about horny monkeys, but these guys wouldn't stop—cute little fellows without tails, and their things were enormous, like franks plumping on the grill. The rats squealed louder but an octave lower than the mice, and the gerbils and hamsters were blurs as they banged away on their little treadmills.

I hate to say that word but it was a fucking circus. And I was so embarrassed, I couldn't speak.

"I've discovered the fountain of sexual youth, Patty." Booly was ecstatic.

"How nice," I said, blushing like a ripe tomato.

"Their erections have not diminished in twelve hours, and you'll note the females are insatiable." He smiled right at me.

"How ni—" I couldn't say it.

One female monkey collapsed in exhaustion, but her smiling mate kept humping the air like a male stripper. I tried not to look at this bestial porn show but I couldn't resist it.

I asked Booly why his snakes were so passive.

"They are my secret, Madam Patty."

"How nice," I said, deciding not to ask about the jar of brown things.

"My quest is to prolong life and to prolong life one needs a reason to live. And what better reason is there than sex and procreation?"

He must know Rex, I thought.

"And to have complete sex," he continued, "the male must be tumescent and remain so throughout the copulative timetable."

I figured he meant "keep it up."

"Voila," he beamed. "I think I've done it." My people will have longer life through greater urge. But one swallow doesn't make a winter as you Americans say. My findings must be tested over long periods of time."

"That makes sense," I said.

What the hell, I thought. The animals would screw themselves to death but they'd be happy. No cause for "Friends of Lab Animals" to be concerned.

Then, thank God, the sexy little maid came in to tell Booly his lunch was ready. I couldn't wait to get out of there.

On the way out I wondered if the maid was helping Booly with his experiments.

The House of Rittenhouse

I DREAMED OF SNAKES humping monkeys, mice humping snakes and Booly humping me. I woke up horrified and embarrassed.

The morning *Journal* had two headline stories:

MANCOTTI URGES SUPERVISORS VOTE TO SHUT DOWN COSMETIC QUACKS and

BELLEVUE PAUNCHE DROPS BIG CLIENT; TARGETS DENTON AND STEINBRENNER

Paunche had been retained by a crazy group in Panama called "U.S.A. Get Out Already," who were suing Donald Trump because his giant new floating hotel and casino had stuck in one of the Canal's locks, stifling all shipping and precluding any new tolls. The rather disorganized group had reneged on Paunche's retainer, however, so he'd dropped the case and was now planning to destroy Denton and Steinbrenner. I'd felt all along the bastard would get in the act.

That morning at 11, I had a date with Mimmsy Rittenhouse. While eating breakfast, the phone rang and I hoped it was Kleindienst, but I was nervous about what he'd say.

"Miz Nottingham?"

"Yes. Mr. Kleindienst?"

"I got it. It's a compound of—"

He rattled off chemical names more complicated than the stuff in Diet Dr. Pepper.

"Great," I said, having no idea what he was talking about.

"Y'better come over. I'll give you a written report."

I figured he wanted his money first.

"Is it poison?"

"Rather not discuss it by phone, lady, but it's stronger than Valium." I imagined his gross brown teeth chuckling over that one.

"Be right over."

"Can't have the report 'til tomorrow," he said.

So I saw Mimmsy.

The exterior of the Rittenhouse mansion looked like a small museum. So did the interior. Mimmsy and Rod had mega-bucks, but were the nicest, most humble of the crowd. The butler who'd let me in reflected their kindness. A sweet old black gentleman who'd probably been with them forever. Mimmsy had walked to the door with the butler to welcome me.

She led me to their library which was bigger than my entire apartment. It was a warm room with walls of books and lots of photographs of family, friends, and parties they'd attended. We sat in comfortable beige corduroy chairs.

Like everyone else, Mimmsy was fiftyish. The prettiest and chicest of all of them; blond with dewy skin and a lovely, but not too scrawny figure. I'm sure she'd had a tuck or two to preserve her lovely face, but everyone did.

"You look lovely, Patty. Wish I had your cute little figure."

She'd noticed. What a dear.

"Thank you, Mimmsy. I've cut down on cheese puffs and alcohol."

"I haven't touched a drop for a year. I feel so much better."

"But you've always had a perfect figure," I said.

"You're so kind."

Her smile was contagious.

She'd remembered about my trend setters article and said

she'd love to help me with it. If they could all have been like dear Mimmsy.

Before talking fashion and interiors, I commented about the party she'd chaired. "Your symphony evening was a smash, Mimmsy."

"Delighted everyone had fun."

"And people were so kind about cute little Phil Toakhime's music. Poor dear tries so hard," she said, winking at me.

I acknowledged her wink.

"I worried about you that evening, Mimmsy."

"Why, my dear?"

"Binky, Neenie and Buffy. All chairwomen of their events. All dead."

"Dreadful, I know dear, but I truly believe those doctors were at fault."

She was sold on the doctor theory, too.

"And their diets," she said. "A bird couldn't live on what they ate."

"You sat with them those evenings, didn't you?"

"Yes and they seemed healthy and happy. Lots of champagne and dancing after dinner. They all stayed after Rod and I left. As chairwomen, I suppose they felt they should remain 'til the end."

So here was another one making the point that each of the three ladies stayed on after the others at their tables had left. And in all cases the victims' husbands, or escort in Neenie's case, had gone for their chauffeurs or their sables.

But why hadn't Mimmsy been killed? She'd given up drinking. Maybe that was why.

I raved over Mimmsy's peach silk pants suit, and she told me she'd designed it.

I asked what she thought of Lamar's designs.

"Fascinating but perhaps he should tone down his creativity a touch."

Better, I thought, for him to tone down his chemical intake.

"Notice anything strange those evenings?" I asked.

She smiled. "You sound like you're investigating a murder."

"Don't you think it's possible, Mimmsy?"

"Why? Why would anyone want to?"

"Jealousy. Envy. Possible hanky panky."

She rose, walked to the doorway and pulled a long, gold silk rope hanging from the ceiling alongside the door. In a few seconds the nice butler arrived to take our drink order.

We both ordered hot tea. Mimmsy had defected from the "Royal Order of bloody mary" some years ago.

"But who, dear? Who could it possibly be?" she asked.

"I wish I knew."

I wanted to suggest it was someone at the table, but until I heard the Kleindienst report, I'd keep quiet. I was suspicious of Lamar, Prudence, Booly and H-M. Just a feeling about H-M . . . the way she'd warned me to forget writing about the deaths. Lamar: His snit about society spurning his gowns, his thing with the flowers and his inflamed nostrils. And Prudence: She wasn't her old self when I interviewed her—or was it a hangover?

"Mimmsy dear, you may think I'm balmy, but please watch carefully everything that goes on at your table at the Opera Ball. You could be the next target as I thought you would be at the Symphony Ball."

"You're so dear. I promise to be careful."

"The food, the flowers, the desserts, the drinks. Be careful. Someone could be using poison."

I sensed she wanted to get off the subject, so we discussed her views on fashion and interior design. She promised to keep our "trend setters" talk confidential. I felt sleazy lying to Mimmsy about my "article," but if nothing else, I'd warned her.

$\triangledown$

That's Some Kind
of Protein

My OLD SCHOOL CHUM Marlowe Tweed, a bookish-looking balding redhead who instructed Criminology II at Berkeley, greeted me cordially and invited me into his tiny office where I sat in a government-style chair by his little grey metal desk.

I'd finally gotten the report from Kleindienst and wanted to find out more. I couldn't understand what Kleindienst was talking about and his report was even worse.

Word was that Marlowe Tweed knew all there was to know about poison.

We small-talked about our undergraduate days. Then I handed him the analysis. He put on his wire-rimmed glasses and read it, nodding his head knowingly at first, but as he read on he looked puzzled.

"Anything unusual, Tweedy?"

"Unique, Patty," he said, continuing to study the report.

Why couldn't it be plain old cyanide or strychnine? Tweedy looked baffled.

"I'm familiar with the components," he said. "But I've never seen them mixed together. Actually they're incompatible."

"Like oil and water?"

"Exactly."

"But it *is* poison?"

"One part is."

"Enough to kill someone?"

"If they ingest enough, yes."

"What's the other part?"

"Don't know exactly, but it's not toxic."

"Harmless?"

"Nothing's harmless, Patty, but it's not poison."

I asked about the poison part.

"It's a complex mixture of proteins."

Sounds like my diet.

"How does it kill?" I asked.

"It's a neurotoxin that works rapidly on the central nervous system."

"Painful?"

"It's instant, as opposed to hemotoxins that attack blood systems causing slower, more painful deaths."

"Where does it come from, Tweedy?"

"Its sources are too numerous to mention. The chemicals can be extracted from flora, fauna or synthetics. There are labs that do incredible computer analyses, but I don't think you'd want to spend that kind of money, Patty."

"You've helped me enough, Tweedy."

It was poison. Period. That was what I wanted to know. The hell with where it came from. The important thing was to be on the scene when the phantom struck the next victim.

The Cruel Sea

THE FEUD BETWEEN SEA OTTER advocates and abalone divers gets hotter every year. Frankly I like sauted abalone, but I feel sorry for the cute little otters.

They weren't nasty enough to serve abalone steak at the "Friends of the Sea Otter" benefit luncheon, but perhaps it was because the otters had almost devoured them out of existence.

To save their business abalone divers had declared war on sea otters and were killing them off with guns, dynamite, nets, anything to get rid of them.

The real socialites avoided these small affairs. They were usually staged by the Vuitton climbing set to get into the social column. Committee chairwoman was Margo Needlebaum, wife of the rich orthodontist. President of the sea otter friends was Bertha Starbuck.

Starbuck, who had permanent scuba marks on her pointy face, practically lived with the little mammals, like the woman with the chimpanzees. Her pruny blue flesh, not covered by her black rubber dress, looked like she'd soaked in a bathtub for days.

I was surprised to see Myra Bamburger of Channel 10 across the room. It had to be a slow news week for her to cover such a silly event.

108

After opening the meeting with two belchy barks—mating call of the male sea otter—Bertha explained that unless we preserve the sea otter the California shoreline will cave in by the year 2,800 and Las Vegas will become a seaport. Then she opened the floor to suggestions.

Someone suggested putting bells around otters' necks to warn the abalones. Bertha pointed out that abalones can't hear under water and even if they could hear they'd have a hell of a time getting unstuck from their rocks in time.

"Ship our sea otters to Monterey Aquarium."

"Muzzle the otters and feed them intravenously."

"Confiscate abalone divers' tire irons."

"Screw the abalone dives."

And on it went. Can't feed the homeless and they were carrying on about that drivel.

My column groupies surrounded me while I made notes after the meeting. Across the room I noticed Myra Bamburger with a seedy little guy, probably her cameraman, coming toward me.

Like many newscasters (they call themselves investigative journalists), Myra suffered from "teleprompter fatigue," a disease caused by overexposure to the newscasters' crutch. Myra's eyes had only one focal point. Instead of looking at me she focused two feet in front of my face and her eyeballs oscillated side-to-side as though she were watching a ping pong game played by mice. Her hands were shuffling invisible papers and she had two robotic facial expressions—a broad smile and a concerned look. Nothing in between.

"Hello Myra, what brings you to this world-shaking event?"

With her look of concern, she said, "Doing a story on our disappearing coastal mammals for tonight's news. Wish I had your cushy job. Free lunches and balls all the time."

"I'll trade you."

As Myra spoke, I saw her assistant roaming around the room taking random footage with a small vidcam.

"How 'bout Bertha Starbuck?" I said. "She even claps like a seal."

"We need more people like that," Myra said, sustaining her concerned look, not thinking I was at all funny.

"I felt terrible about the three lovely women you always wrote about," she said, changing the subject.

"At least they went out smiling," I said.

"Those doctors should be put away."

"I don't believe the doctors had anything to do with—"
Big mouth me. I knew I shouldn't have said that.

"Think there was foul play, Patty?"

"Could be," I said. "But I'd rather not comment on it, Myra. O.K.?"

She tried to talk more about it, but I said it was nice to see her again and that I had to get to my office.

$\bigtriangledown$

Trapped

ALL COMFY ON MY couch. I turned on Channel 10's
evening news. A rape, an oily duck from a tanker spill and
then Myra Bamburger. Instead of reporting the sea otter
thing she began a feature called "Balls of Death" and I saw
a closeup of myself among the sea otter crowd saying I didn't
think the doctors had anything to do with it and that it could
be foul play.

She had trapped me. Probably had a tape recorder in her
purse and her assistant had used a zoom to isolate me. The
sneaky bitch was doing a story on *my* case.

I knew then I'd had it with H-M, and Peter couldn't save
me again.

Next morning, while I was writing about the great sea
otter/abalone dilemma, Peter called me to his office. When
Peter called me to *his* office it was always bad news.

He told me he loved me but how stupid was I to get taken
in by Myra Bamburger?

"It was a polite chat," I said, "Myra told me she was doing
a series on disappearing sea mammals. I didn't know she
was recording me, and I thought they were videotaping the
meeting for her feature.

"And you believed that horseshit?" Peter said. "Channel

111

10 doesn't cover anything less than murder or a gay parade."
Whenever Peter said horseshit, I knew he was upset.

"H-M's already told me to have you clean out your desk,"
he said, unable to look at me.

"It *is* a mess," I said, injecting a little humor because Peter
was on the verge of tears.

His phone rang and he picked it up. "I told you already,"
he shouted. "Run the story on Michael Jackson buying
Plains, Georgia . . . and no one cares if Barry Manilow's
mother is in town—"

Editing our entertainment section was really too much for
Peter.

He slammed down the phone and looked at me. "Don't
you care at all, Patty? The Opera Ball's coming up and I have
no one to cover it."

"What about Gerald Boswell?"

"Good idea, but he can only see in the dark."

$\triangledown$

The Celebrity

"**Y**OU'RE A DEAR, PETER. I'll never forget y—"

"Just don't make anymore dumb remarks about your Binky-Buffy crowd."

I gave him a big hug. I could feel he was choked up.

H-M had given me a reprieve. To save me Peter warned H-M of the embarrassing publicity her *Journal* would suffer over the union fighting my dismissal and told her he had no one to cover the Opera Ball.

"Even Rudolph Junior wanted to dump you," Peter said.

I wasn't surprised. Junior thought my column was a waste of valuable space and hated the society crowd.

"We need an old pro like you to cover the Opera Ball," Peter said, which I thought was flattering except for the "old" part.

I had to face it, though. I was on probation. I decided to make a couple of advance rent payments in case I got axed after the big ball.

A slow week. No events to report and it was tough to put out a column without an affair to feature. So I called a lot of people, asked who'd been where, who was in town, where they'd had lunch, who was divorced, traveling, and so on. My Rolodex had gossips who usually came through.

The next column I wrote was pure drivel:

PATTIE'S CHATTER

DOODIE AND GRAMM HARKNESS LIMO'D TO PEBBLE TO STAY AT PUSSY AND BIFF STRANGEL-SMITH'S NEW GUEST COTTAGE, DECORATED BY LAMONT McFLY. OUR CREATIVE LITTLE PUSSY CALLS IT HER 'NINETEENTH HOLE'.

APPROPRIATE BECAUSE IT'S BUILT ENTIRELY OF GOLF BALLS BIFF FOUND ON HIS PROPERTY BORDERING CYPRESS POINT'S EIGHTEENTH HOLE. BIFF'S BEEN BUSY COLLECTING GOLF BALLS FOR FIFTEEN YEARS AND GLAD IT'S OVER. NOW WE KNOW WHEN BIFF ALWAYS SAID HE WAS HAVING A BALL, HE WASN'T KIDDING. PUSSY SAYS THE GUEST HOUSE LOOKS LIKE A DELICIOUS MOUND OF POPCORN. . . .

THEY BROKE OUT THE FINLANDIA VODKA LAST NIGHT AT KINKY AND DRUMMOND BRIDGE-HAVEN'S MANSION, HONORING FINLAND'S NEW MINISTER OF ALCOHOL AND DRUG CONTROL, TRYGVE FJORDSTAD, WHO ARRIVED LAST NIGHT ON AIR FINNISH. ON HAND TO TOAST TRYGVE AND SING A ROUSING CHORUS OF 'FINLANDIA' WERE BABSY AND HUNT ROCKRIDGE, BUNKY AND BRAD RIDGEROCK, BOOPSY AND ROCK STOCKBRIDGE, BUMMSY AND HUCK BRECKENRIDGE, DINKY AND RIDLEY HUNTING-HOUSE, MIMMSY AND RODMAN RITTENHOUSE, SHOTSIE FENNER AND HUNTLEY HAVERSTOCK, PRUDY AND BOOLY JABBAR-LAMUMBA. . . .

I finished the column and on my way home stopped at one of our Arab corner grocery stores. I picked out a head of Iceberg lettuce, two tomatoes and a bunch of green onions. I was still dieting for Rex.

I said hello to Omar, standing by a little wooden money drawer he called his "tax shelter." Omar's mouth featured a perpetual sneering smile of saliva-coated teeth that reminded me of a camel waiting to be fed its dates.

"My famous customer," he said. "Tonight I geev you lettuce free."

I looked around, thinking he was talking to someone else. Omar pointed to his rack of *Playboys, Hustlers and Intruders*. The new *Intruder*'s cover featured my face bigger than life. The bold red headline read:

"UNTOLD SECRET OF SOCIETY SCRIBE— FRISCO'S FANCY FEMS FINISHED BY FANTOM, says Frisco *Journal*'s Patty Nottingham."

Stunned, I couldn't speak for a moment.

"Thanks Omar," I quivered. "You're sweet. I'll take a pint of brandy too."

"Brandy and sahlad. Nice deener." He smile-sneered, reaching up for a dusty pint of Christian Brothers brandy.

He put the things in a bag. I gave him a ten dollar bill and grabbed an *Intruder*.

"Also I geev you onions. Celebration. You pay only tomatoes, newspaper and brandy."

"Thanks Omar." I started to cry, and he thought I was undone with happiness at being a celebrity.

He put my ten dollar bill in his pocket, gave me change from his little drawer and said, "Goodbye my famous customer."

In my Datsun outside Omar's, I snapped through the pages of Maximillian Pinkus' filthy rag to get to my article. Typical tabloid. Creative lying. Said I knew who killed Binky, Neenie and Buffy and that I wouldn't tell so I could keep my job. That the snobby Huntting-Margates wanted no social scandals, etcetera, etcetera.

Nobody believes their trash, but God they sure read it. Everyone who goes through a grocery check out line. H-M had never stood in a checkout line, but I knew damn well she'd read that issue.

Set Adrift

W<small>HEN</small> P<small>ETER</small> W<small>ROTE</small> M<small>E</small> notes in shaky handwriting it was big trouble. On my desk was a note saying "Please come see me at once, Peter."

"This is it, Patty," he said, sucking short gulps of air like a hurt child about to cry. "Clean out your desk."

"Is it dirty again?" I smiled, trying to make it easier.

"Don't make it tougher on me," he said, avoiding eye contact fearing he'd break down.

"I'll miss you, Peter."

"It's not your fault, Patty, I know."

With his hands over his face, he began sobbing like a baby.

I kissed the back of his head and walked to my cubicle where I wrote a quick memo to him thanking him for all he'd done for me.

Misery. I had no job. Rex was in New York probably sleeping with his ex-wife to stall alimony payments, and some creep was planning to cremate me if I didn't stop my investigation.

That evening a yellow slip with the final warning to pick up the registered letter from the Manhattan zip was in my mailbox. Probably a check from Pinkus and if I accepted it, the *Intruder* would be off the hook. Not that the *Intruder* worried much about law suits, but the *Journal* could make it difficult for them.

I thought if it was a check, I'd accept it. Why not? I was dead in the water anyway, and I'd need money to live on if I couldn't get a job right away.

Next morning I drove to my Post Office on Fillmore Street. The registered letter contained a $5,000 check and a memo from Maximillian Pinkus promising $20,000 more if I'd submit to an interview and photo session for follow-up stories.

$5,000 would help 'til I got a job, but I thought I'd hold off promising an interview until after I found the murderer. Then I could ask for a lot more than $20,000. I expected Pinkus to be on my back after he heard I took the check, so I thought about taking him up on an elegant dinner date. A nice change from Rex's Jack-in-the-Box takeouts.

Word spread fast and calls came in from all over about jobs. First was *Our Crowd*—the little throw-away society paper. Then the *Oakland Post* and the papers from Fresno, Sacramento and some small valley towns. I imagined writing up the *Haute Monde* of Modesto.

I had to stay in San Francisco, and while it paid peanuts, *Our Crowd* was my choice. My ticket to catch the murderer of San Francisco's thoroughbreds.

Pammie Quackenbush, who needs a job like a hole in the head, publishes *Our Crowd*, which loses money that husband "Ducky" writes off. The Quackenbush family owns half the financial district, and are the ones who built the Zoo and Aquarium.

Pammie believed my story and was thrilled to get me away from Mrs. Huntting-Margate whom she didn't particularly care for.

Except for not wearing white sheets and pointed hats, *Our Crowd*'s staff reminded me of the Social Register, the way they shunned "undesireables." Editors used large rubber stamps with the letters DNOC to delete commoners' photos from appearing in their silly little paper. DNOC meaning "definitely not our class." As I mentioned, *Our Crowd* publishes nothing but social events with pictures of the "in" crowd. Society's monthly masturbator.

But I figured the little rag would at least get me into the Opera Ball.

Had I been fired under normal conditions, people wouldn't have cared that much, but the media grabbed the story because of my recent notoriety. Not an *Intruder* was left on the stands and I was big news with the local television, radio and newspapers. They were all begging me for interviews. Even the national press was starting to talk about little old me.

$\bigtriangledown$

Olé

ON CHANNEL 10'S SIX o'clock news, Myra Bamburger continued her "Balls of Death" feature and made a big thing about my leaving the *Journal*, mentioning I knew more than I would say. Myra thought it was murder and berated the police for not pursuing it beyond Doctors Denton and Steinbrenner.

I called her after the show, warning her not to use my name anymore in her feature. Snotty as ever, she countered with the bill of rights, freedom of the press, and her duty as a journalist. I told her to shove it in her earpiece.

If she'd only known I had the weapon.

The Channel 6 eleven o'clock news blasted a special report on Denton and Steinbrenner. Police had traced the poor chaps to Salsarita, a suburb of Mexico City, where they'd set up a clinic. A perfect spot for Steinbrenner because women down there devour tons of refried beans, blowing up at early ages to nearly the girth of Sumo wrestlers. Steinbrenner'd already worn out two liposuction pumps and that's how they'd traced him. When he reordered pumps from the *Trimphat Pump Company* in Newport Beach, California, the order clerk recognized Steinbrenner's name from news reports and called the police.

Dr. Denton was a mess. Salsarita women didn't wrinkle

until they were eighty and by then their mates had died of tequila rot, an insidious disease not unlike the French liver problem. Denton's "lift" business was nada, and he'd surrendered to alcohol. Steinbrenner had begged him to learn liposuction, but Denton thought it beneath his art.

Lieutenant Kilarney claimed that extradition papers would bring Denton and Steinbrenner to San Francisco for trial very shortly.

Newscaster Ben Wong thanked Kilarney, shuffled a few papers and said "goodnight from Channel 6 where the news is—"

Two loud crashes through glass—one through my bedroom window, followed by another through my television set at the foot of the bed. When the smoke from the television set cleared I saw something wrapped in yellow paper inside the set. Using a towel from the bathroom I pulled out a thing about the size of a small cantaloupe. A rock wrapped in paper. Like in the movies again.

I should have stayed in Rex's apartment as he suggested.

$\triangledown$

Expensive Trip

I REMOVED THE PAPER from the rock and read the note:

MIND YOUR OWN BUSINESS AND YOU WON'T GET HURT

That's all it said, printed in primitive block letters with a red magic marker on legal pad paper.

Scared to death, I drove to Rex's to spend the night and had a dreadful time falling asleep, re-living the rock thing, feeling invaded . . . violated, frightened . . . and furious at the thought of buying a new television set and having to fix my window.

The *Our Crowd* office was located in a double suite in the Fairmont Hotel. Imagine the rent. Pammie Quackenbush welcomed me and we talked about upcoming events. The Gaeties Ball had been postponed 'til after the Opera Ball. Eddy Frecker's hot New York band couldn't make the date, Eddy having fractured his right pinky at the Boy's Club ball at the Plaza.

So I had time to concentrate on my strategy for catching the murderer at the Opera Ball.

Pammie skittered around like a blond waterbug handing out assignments. My first was a fashion show featuring a

121

young designer sponsored by Sophie Jacobs who by now had spent half her fortune climbing into *Our Crowd*'s beau monde.

Pammie's staff was fairly cordial—kind of a forced politeness. I suppose some felt threatened by my big newspaper background in their dumb business. My deal was to work freelance, so I'd have even more loose time than at the *Journal*. More freedom, less money.

The fashion show featured "breakthrough" designs by Marcel Sparrowbush, who in his pillow-ticking jump suit floated among the guests like a delicate grey cloud. (He and Lamar Philbin could have been bookends). Sophie Jacobs had found an underground cosmetic surgeon and now looked like Bette Davis in a Prince Valiant wig. All smiles, caviar balls between her teeth, she greeted me. I always stood a safe distance from Sophie because she sprayed tiny bits of hors d'oeuvres toppings and Carr's water biscuits when she spoke.

Eddie, my loyal freelance photographer, was at my side snapping away. Pammie loved scads of pictures of the right people drinking and smiling at each other.

After the show I went back to *Our Crowd* and typed my column and photo captions, then took the elevator down to get my car. Simpson, the Fairmont doorman, had parked my Datsun for me. He never forgot when I wrote about him in Pattie's Chatter.

Rex called that evening and asked me to meet United Airlines flight 23 arriving 10:30 the next morning, lower level. Thank God, I really missed him. Rex didn't sound too happy.

The airport police kept chasing me as I tried to park at the United Airlines "Arrivals" section, and I circled for half an hour 'til Rex—in his traveling navy Bogner warmup suit—finally walked through the automatic sliding doorway. Seeing him sent that pleasant little twinge to my lower half. But Rex didn't look that thrilled. He had a forced smile on his face. I got out of the car, we hugged and kissed, put his suitcase in the trunk, and headed for the city.

"Seems you've been gone for months," I said, squeezing his hand.

"Seems longer than that."

"Everything all right?" I knew it wasn't.

"When we were divorced, New York was really tough on alimony settlements."

"So?" I hated to pry, but. . . .

"She had me subpoenaed when I got off the plane. Her lawyer arranged a court hearing for the day after I got there."

"Poor baby."

"I shouldn't have gone."

Sounded bad. I shut up.

"Got me for nine thousand in back payments."

"Jesus." I had to say something strong to acknowledge the horror.

Passing *Candlestick Park*, he kissed my cheek and said, "Let's drop it for now. Tell me what's happening."

"I got the Kleindienst report."

"Sounds like a Senate hearing."

"The Oakland chemist. Remember?"

He smiled. "I know, sweetie, just kidding."

"It's poison."

"Great . . . I mean, well at least it's not Jello."

"The report's home in my douche bag."

"In your what?" he said, laughing.

"I figured it's the last place anyone would look."

"I'll buy that," he said. "What kind of—"

"Of poison?"

"Yeah, is it bad stuff?"

"Part of it is. I took the report to a friend of mine at Berkeley who teaches Criminology II. He says it's a neurotoxin that attacks the central nervous system. Like fast."

"Part of it?"

"Marlowe says one part's not poison."

"What's neurotoxin?"

"A complex mixture of proteins."

"Come on—"

"That's what I thought, but chemicals are crazy."

"I flunked chemistry."

"Marlowe says the poison could be from flora, fauna or synthetics and that a sophisticated, expensive computer analysis could identify its source, but I said forget it. It's deadly poison. That's enough."

"Who's Marlowe?"

"My friend at Berkeley. I just told you."

"Of course. Sorry. Let's go to your place."

Rather than spoil his airport homecoming with my troubles, I waited 'til we got to my apartment to tell him how I got fired and about the rock.

▽

Move Over Eddy Frecker

IF REX HAD BEEN sleeping with his ex-wife, he was superman because he had me nailed to the bed non-stop for an hour and a half, at least. My new frosted hairdo looked like wet seaweed. But it was divine, as Shotsie Fenner would say.

Sitting on the couch later in our white terry robes, I told Rex why I'd been fired, about my job at *Our Crowd* and about the rock with the note. Then I showed him the *Intruders* and other articles in the press and told him about the television reports and bitch Myra Bamburger.

"I'm worried, Patty. I don't want you hurt. Better move into my place, and I'll move into yours. Maybe I can catch the son of a bitch."

Then he brought up his alimony problem. "So where do I get nine thousand bucks?"

"You'll work it out," I said, knowing he was down to his last cummerbund.

"I can't even buy you a nice dinner. And someday you'll be off your diet."

"You're not my meal ticket, Rex. I love you." First time I'd said I loved him and I hoped it wouldn't scare him to death.

I was hoping he'd say he loved me too, but I knew men hated to say that. I read it years ago in *Redbook*.

125

"Why not start your own band, dear?" I'd thought of it before, but hadn't wanted to appear pushy. Now he needed more money.

"You kidding?"

"No, you've got the talent and charisma."

He liked that.

"I've never led a band."

"Neither had fat little Eddy Frecker, but look at him. Makes a fortune banging the piano unmercifully and sweating out his wee wee so he can play all night without stopping."

"I don't want to do that, for Godsakes."

"You missed my point, dear. I'm just saying you've got more talent and you're handsome. You can develop a style."

"I'll need arrangements," he said, showing a little interest.

"Sherman Clay's music store's got thousands of them for a few bucks each. You can doctor the notes a little."

"How do I get gigs?"

"With my connections I'll get you lots of jobs . . . gigs. You can have a big band like Bernie Hellman's to play the charity balls. Maybe take Bernie's place eventually. Bernie could barely lift his baton at the Deb ball."

I'd motivated him and he looked excited—excited for Rex, that is. The only time I saw him really excited was in bed.

"All right I'll try it," he said. "As long as I can go to the bathroom once in a while."

"My hero."

"I'll keep my job at the Mark Hopkins while I start calling musicians. The union will help."

"You'll be America's new Peter Duchin," I beamed.

"I'll pay off my alimony, buy a Steinway for 'Gershwin' and get a bigger apartment."

Then he kissed me and said, "And you'll be rich and famous when you catch the murderer."

I was hoping he'd say, "and then we can get married."

$\bigtriangledown$

Myra's Mission

I LET REX SLEEP as I quietly dressed, got the morning *Journal* from outside my door and went into the kitchen. After starting my Mr. Coffee, I reached into the freezer for my fake bacon next to the sugar-free lemon sorbet container in which I'd recently hidden the poison stuff, having transferred it from my douche bag. (Not that Rex liked lemon sorbet, but I warned him about it just in case.)

I dropped my frying pan when the front page caught my eye: A huge picture of Denton and Steinbrenner in handcuffs and with heads bowed to avoid photographers. The red banner headline said:

"STRETCH" DENTON AND "NON-FAT" STEIN-BRENNER BACK FROM MARGARITAVILLE. Sub-head: "Cosmetic-cutups to stand trial for Ball Deaths."

A nauseating quote from Lieutenant Kilarney followed: "Our tireless pursuit paid off, and now we'll balance the scales of justice when these irresponsible quacks are put behind bars." Later in the article the reporter quoted Bellevue Paunche as saying he'd sue for malpractice. "We can't bring back life to the ashes of Binky, Neenie and Buffy," Paunche said. "But we'll compensate their loved ones for suffering such agonizing grief." (And Paunche would get eighty percent.)

127

I finished breakfast and left a note for Rex saying I'd be at *Our Crowd* for a couple of hours, then at an art showing at Bellingford's on Sutter Street and would see him later that afternoon.

Rene Brie's art statements entitled *Litterwaste Mania I,* were clusters of things on giant sheets of brown wrapping paper: Cigarette butts, used scouring pads, theater stubs, worn-out golf gloves, McDonald's hamburger containers, broken light bulbs, and so on. I'd never understood this art, but everyone was oohing and ahhing over it.

Rene, swarthily handsome and always dressed impeccably is a shrewd promoter and refreshingly "straight." Ladies wet their pants over Rene, who I'm sure goes along as a bonus with many art pieces he sells. I'd seen him at lots of parties.

Besides his "cluster" period, Brie showed a series called "Life." First was a single poppy seed glued in the center of a four-by-eight piece of plywood, entitled "Beginning." The second, also on plywood, was a broken eggshell with a feather sticking out of it, called "Almost." Another was a mounted condom with a hole in its end, called "Broken Promise." A large, mounted penus bone from a sperm whale, called "Life's Harpoon," sold for $50,000 to Boopsy Stockbridge who had to have it for her Aptos beach house.

Rex had gone to work when I got back, so I sat down and read the evening *Examiner*—another huge story on Denton and Steinbrenner. They'd put poor Dr. Denton in the prison de-tox section to "neutralize his tequila saturated body tissues." And apparently the re-fried bean set in Salsarita had made Steinbrenner rich but he'd never get to spend it. Police confiscated millions of pesos he'd stashed in two serapes and three Mexican straw hats in his bedroom. Their trial, it said, would be held January 13, a week prior to the Opera Ball.

Local television news people were orgasmic. Every channel

showed videotapes of the doctors pushed like animals through crowds into a police van with caged windows. Lieutenant Kilarney's face invaded the camera, answering reporters' questions, taking credit for "apprehending the perps" and promising to "balance the scale of justice."

Channel 10's Lathrup Truss and Myra Bamburger did their teleprompter duet of the six o'clock news, dominated by the doctors' extradition story. Following the news portion Myra continued her "Balls of Death" feature. This, of course, was her editorial opinion and not that of Channel 10 or its holding company, Consolidated Oil, Gas and Lumber Corporation.

Myra pushed her theory about murder, telling us a mad killer was still at large, and she accused "over-age-in-grade" Lieutenant Kilarney of pushing for a promotion and the police department for neglecting to investigate alternatives.

"The easy way out," she said. "The police department just wants to close the case—get it over with. They don't care if the accused are innocent."

"Or am I being unfair?" she said. "Perhaps our invisible Mayor should try to raise the morale of our police instead of raising money by selling their horses to Alpo."

"No matter what," she said. "Our Homicide Department should be ashamed of itself."

In the back of my sometimes cynical little mind, I had thought Myra might be the one invading my apartment. But hearing her views on Kilarney, I was beginning to like her.

She was right about a killer on the loose, and I couldn't let her beat me to it. With her big TV audience, she'd have everyone in the Bay Area looking for the murderer.

But I was still a big step ahead—I had the weapon.

$\triangledown$

Left Hooked

WE EXCHANGED APARTMENTS AND Rex took Gershwin with him, thank God. I loved the little bird but his singing was too much of a good thing.

Rex's place was a pig pen, but I cleaned it up and made do. I didn't have to use his gross kitchen much. I ate out a lot because of my assignments for Our Crowd which covered ten times more things than the Journal—every little cocktail party, dinner party, dance, tea, bridge party, boat trip, picnic . . . . We reported every trip and vacation and if we didn't cover it, readers sent in their own pictures and captions . . . subject, of course, to our DNOC rubber stamp.

One good thing about working for *Our Crowd*: I had plenty of job connections for Rex's new band which he'd been rehearsing almost every day at the musicians union hall. He told me he had something totally different from the other local bands. He wouldn't tell me what though . . . he wanted to surprise me at his first "gig." One thing he did tell me: since the trend was non-stop playing with no intermissions, he'd gotten a bass player who could also play the piano so he could go to the bathroom one in a while.

It was a Tuesday evening and I was scheduled to cover a white tie do held in the ballroom of Pussy and Biff Stranglesmith's mansion on Russian Hill, honoring former Prince Helmut Blattwurster, undisputed croquet champion of Austria. Cleverly called the "Croquet Ball," the party's theme was carried out with astroturf surrounding the dance floor, including wickets so guests could knock around a few balls between dances. Cute idea, but people were tripping on the wickets. Old Bitsy Longtree re-broke her hip and was taken to St. Francis Hospital, prompting Pussy to remove the wickets and call off the croquet playing.

Rex was waiting for me when I got home—to his apartment, not mine—and I noticed his entire left hand was bandaged.

"You must've really wowed them tonight," I said, hoping it wasn't serious.

"I was about to leave your apartment for work when your friend Pinkus buzzed from the lobby and asked me out to dinner. I faked a girl voice and told him to come up."

"Oh my God." Rex has a terrible temper and for fiftyish he's still very strong.

"I let the fat bastard in and he asked where you were, thinking I was your father I guess, with my grey hair and all, and I said here she is . . . *POW*, and belted him with my best left hook, which I learned as a boxer in the army."

"And you hurt him badly?"

"Just his face, which I couldn't see too well because it was covered with blood from his big greasy nose."

"And he ran out?"

"He was already out."

"Cold?"

"Hit the floor like a stuffed body bag."

"Oh dear." Deep trouble from the *Intruder*, I was thinking.

"Gershwin sang through the whole thing."

"So tell me the worst."

"While he's still out I shook ketchup all over his crotch. Maybe it was chili sauce. It was red anyway. Hope you don't mind my using it."

"You forgot onions. They were in the vegetable drawer."

"I threw a potful of water on his face and he started mumbling."

"Then?"

"I told him to leave my daughter alone, or I'd kill him and that I'd already cut his dick off."

"Oh dear. And then?"

"He reached down into the ketchup and fainted."

"And then?"

"More water and by now Gershwin's doing his piercing high note vibrating number and Pinkus comes out of it."

"I know that sound of Gershwin's."

"Pinkus finally gets up and tears out the door, looking like he's been in a Cuisinart. You won't hear from that schmuck again."

"My hero." I hugged him and without thinking, grabbed his bandaged hand.

"I'm sorry, dear," I said.

"It's not that bad."

"How can you play the piano?"

"I hit him with a left hook instead of a right cross because I figured I could still play the melody with my right hand and bang a few bass notes with my bandage. Most of those clowns are so drunk they don't know the difference."

I got a bowl of hot salt water so he could soak his hand.

$\triangledown$

The Well Hung Jury

THEY SQUEEZED IN THE Denton/Steinbrenner trial early
due to a postponement of the unprecedented "Meter Maid
Basher" case. A crazed victim of countless parking tickets,
pretending to be a blind man, had trained a seeing-eye
German Shepherd to terrorize meter maids as they slipped
tickets under windshield wipers, and Pets Unlimited was
doing its damndest to keep "Blitzen" from being put on trial.

The D.A. had subpoenaed me as a witness for the trial of
the City and county of San Francisco vs. Doctors Clinton
Denton and Clyde Steinbrenner, who were charged with
something like improper negligent treatment of three normal healthy patients resulting in death.

A group of Myra Bamburger's viewers, supporting her
"Balls of Death" theory, had formed "Friends of Denton and
Steinbrenner" and plastered reward posters all over the city:
$10,000 REWARD FOR INFORMATION LEADING TO
THE ARREST OF "BALLS OF DEATH" KILLER.

Outside City Hall, where the trial was held, Fannie Doer-
flinger led protesters carrying signs: POISON KILLER
LOOSE! FREE DENTON & STEINBRENNER! FIRE OUR
LAZY COPS!

They were pushing the poison theory, but they had no
evidence. Little did they know that it was in my lemon sorbet

133

where it would stay until I caught the murderer and could use it as proof to convict him, or her . . . or them.

I was on the stand the first day.

We all stood when old Judge Lazlo Barolla came in, and the games began. Because of the deficit left by the former mayor, the doctors were being tried together. Barolla, a bald guy with a fat face full of red veins, explained that the court had appointed a public defender for the doctors. Jesus Mindinao, a young Filipino gentleman, stood up, smiled, bowed and in dreadful English spoke far too many words of welcome to the court audience. His sincere but improper procedure irritated the judge, who raised his gavel, cutting Jesus short.

They'd confiscated Steinbrenner's pesos in Mexico, but I'd heard through a friend of Mrs. Steinbrenner's that the doctor had mailed a stash home to his wife in a large stuffed iguana he'd bought from a taxidermist in Mexico City. He'd opened the large lizard, inserted a few million pesos in its underbelly and sutured it shut. His note enclosed with the souvenir gift said, "This old iguana's too fat from rich food. Love, Clyde." His savvy wife got the clue and removed the pesos. She was also savvy enough to exchange the pesos for travelers checks, file for divorce and take off for Marbella, leaving Clyde without a dime for legal fees.

Except for his baggy orange jump suit, Steinbrenner looked pretty good, but Dr. Denton reminded me of Howard Hughes in his Las Vegas period.

The jury, unchallenged by Mindinao, who hadn't been given time to ask questions, consisted of twelve men who looked like they could use the duty money.

District Attorney Stavros Feta asked me only two questions: Did I know Binky, Buffy and Neenie and did I know they'd retained Denton and Steinbrenner for cosmetic surgery. I said I knew the ladies because of my job, but couldn't swear to their retaining the accused. (Feta later showed surgery invoices as exhibit evidence, so they didn't need my corroboration anyway).

Public defender Mindinao—this was obviously his first case and he was scared out of his gourd—approached me on the stand and asked, "You know Señors Denton and Steinbrenner?"

"Not personally," I said.

With that he bowed and began to introduce me to the doctors sitting at the defendant's table. "Señor Denton and Señor Steinbrenner, may I introduce you to Miss—"

Banging his gavel, Judge Barolla yelled, "This is a trial, counselor, not a reception at the Hilton."

Mindinao apologized, bowed and as a friendly gesture looked up at the judge and said, "Have a nice day."

Steamed at such lack of decorum, the judge mumbled, "Jesus Christ," to himself, not expecting to be heard.

Mindinao smiled up at the judge and said, "That's pronounced 'Haysoos', judge."

Too incensed to go on, Barolla called a ten minute recess.

District Attorney Feta, a swarthy, dapper little man, bombarded the court with expert witnesses, testimony from coroners, neurologists, the deceased's family physicians, crematorium operators, police, Lieutenant Kilarney and a parade of freaky cosmetic surgery victims. The jury was buying every bit of it.

I saw the parasite of malpractice, Bellvue Paunche, sitting in the back drooling at the possibilities.

Mindinao had no witnesses. He'd been appointed the day before the trial began— a week after he passed the bar—and hadn't had time to study the case.

It reminded me of those trials for poor blacks in bigoted southern towns—a real railroad job. In less than a week, Denton and Steinbrenner were pronounced guilty of first degree "womanslaughter." (With pressure from the board of supervisors, the local ACLU and San Francisco's "Friends of Women" organization, our courts now genderize the crime according to sex of the victim. Another San Francisco innovation.) The doctors' medical licenses were revoked and each was given twenty years.

$\bigtriangledown$

Musical Cleavage

REX WAS DYING FOR me to hear his orchestra which he called "The Great Looking Sound." He was booked at the Junior League Fashion Show—his first job.

The new Junior Leaguers looked like sexy children and I felt like their mother. Way at the other end of the ballroom Rex's band had finished tuning up, but I couldn't see them because the model runway was in front of my table. He started playing his theme song, "Body and Soul," which brought tears to my eyes. I got up, pushed through the crowd and there he was—Rex at his piano, leading twelve gorgeous blond musicians in black evening gowns with necklines to their navels. That's what the lech had meant by great looking sound. And not a one over thirty. My tears dried fast.

At 1 A.M. we left the Fairmont Hotel in my Datsun. Rex raved about how great everyone thought his new band was and when he stopped talking I didn't say a word.

"So why so quiet?" he asked. "You don't like my band?"

"You must love rehearsals," I said.

"They're O.K.—except some of them don't show up when they have their periods."

"At least they're not pregnant."

"You're right, I never thought of that."

"Where the hell did you find these women?"

"You'd be surprised how many female musicians are in this area. Most of mine want symphony work, but those jobs are scarce."

"And you had to get all women?"

He finally figured out what was wrong and leaned over to kiss my cheek. I pulled away.

"I thought you'd be thrilled, putting so many women to work. You're always bitching about it's a man's world—"

"I hate it, but it's a good idea."

"You're jealous. Don't be like a woman."

"What do you want me to be like?"

"You know what I mean—"

"Hate to say it, but they play great."

"Thanks, I got the idea reading about this guy Phil Spitalny who had an all girl band back in the forties."

"They look funny playing trombones," I said.

"At least I don't have an accordian player."

"You're a pisser," I said. "But I love you."

"So you like the band?"

"It's wonderful, but keep your long fingers off them."

$\triangledown$

Love at the Eiffel Tower

"F RIENDS OF DENTON AND Steinbrenner" raised money
for an attorney to take the doctors' case, but not enough for
their exorbitant bail so they remained in jail, hoping for an
appeal date before the next Halley's comet.

The Opera Ball was only a week away.

Meanwhile Rex's new band was a sensation, and I plugged
it in my *Our Crowd* column whenever I could. H-M had
copyrighted PATTIE'S CHATTER so I changed it to:

> *PATTIE'S PATTER Our Crowd January, 1990*
> . . . AND REX MURPHY'S NEW BAND CAUSED
> A SENSATION, WITH TWELVE GORGEOUS
> YOUNG WOMEN REVEALING MORE THAN MU-
> SICAL TALENT, PLAYING NONSTOP—

Rex had bookings through June already, with music to fit
any occasion—his twelve piece band, a five piece group, a
trio, and solo piano. His back alimony payments were
whittling down. At least that was what he said.

He spent too much time rehearsing though. I wasn't
seeing enough of him, and I hoped it was all rehearsing. We
did see each other more in the evenings though because he
wasn't playing every night as he had at the Mark Hopkins.

One night he actually took me to a real restaurant, with

a menu and wine list. One of those new trying-to-be-chic but missing South of Market Street numbers called, Le Tower Eiffel. I was smoking again, so the maitre de—complete with fake French accent—stuck us at a table by the kitchen door with a noisy exhaust fan over our heads.

Across the room I saw *Journal* gossip columnist Bert Walker stuffing himself with snails. Bert covers every new place that opens and has never paid for a meal in his life.

I told Rex how sweet he was to take me to such a lovely place, but that I still loved his take-out dinners, implying that he shouldn't be spending too much money until he paid off that woman in New York.

He couldn't hear me over the exhaust fan, so I repeated it, raising my voice louder than the fan.

"You deserve it, sweetheart," he shouted, holding up his straight-up gin martini in toast. "Without you I'd still be playing for convention drunks."

"Without your talent, I couldn't have done anything," I shouted back, clinking his glass with my gimlet, hoping to God his gorgeous women musicians had nice young boyfriends and didn't care for older men.

Then I took a deep, nervous breath. What I was about to ask Rex to do could be a true test of love.

I put my tiny hand across the table and squeezed the beautiful long piano fingers of his masculine hand, the one that wasn't holding the martini and yelled, "If you don't care to, I'll understand and still love you."

"What'd you say?" he yelled back. "I can't hear with this fucking fan."

Other diners turned their heads toward our table.

"Wait a second," he said, getting up and walking to the maitre de' to complain about the fan, pointing to it and using what looked like nasty language until the little man turned it off.

"You'll still love me if I don't what?" he said, sitting back down. "What'd I do now?"

"You did nothing, dear. I've just had a wonderful idea about how you can help me catch the murderer."

"Sounds awful, the way you're leading up to it."

"At the Opera Ball you'll be a waiter."

"You're kidding—"

"You can hover around Mimmsy's table and watch every move. Eddie and I'll be at the next table. We'll be a team of three."

"Team of three, shit. Me a waiter? Comeon," he said, taking a gulp of his martini.

"You needn't shout. The fan's off," I said. "Eddie'll have a small Sony vidcam with his other camera."

"The other waiters would know I'm a phony."

"Not at the Opera Ball. They hire extra waiters from all over for that night."

"What night?"

"Next Thursday."

"I'm playing that night, thank God."

Acting as though I hadn't heard him, I said, "My big chance to be famous as you said—"

"What time would you need me?"

"From 9 on."

"My job starts at 8."

"You could start the band off and leave."

"They'll miss me at the piano."

"Didn't you hire a bass player who can play piano when you go to the bathroom?"

"You don't miss a beat."

I hated asking Rex to skip a job, being so new at the band business and all, but catching the murderer was a case of life or death. My life as much as Mimmsy Rittenhouse's.

"You can be sick all of a sudden," I said. "You're getting on in years; they'll understand."

"Thanks a lot."

I knew what the waiters would wear that night. The committee had chosen maroon dinner jackets, yellow dress shirts and maroon bow ties, all available at the Pronto Uniform Rental Company on Mission Street. I told him I'd already reserved a 44 extra long and 16-1/2 neck size and he could pick it up the day before.

"You little sneak," he said, screening the lemon peel with his sparkling white teeth as he drained his second martini.

"Will you do it?"

"For sexual favors." He smiled in his usual dirty way.

"You're on," I said. "Can you wait 'till we get home?"

"Always a catch," he said.

Our Escalopes de Veau a l'Estragon suffered from l'Estragon overkill, but who cared? Rex had taken me to a real restaurant instead of Jack-in-the-Box. And I knew he must love me to agree to the waiter thing. Not only was he putting himself in danger, but it would be the first time he'd wear something besides black tie or warmup suit.

Later that night as we sat on his gross couch in his so-called living room, he announced he was renting a larger apartment.

For us, I hoped.

Who

No MORE RANSACKING OR rock throwing since we'd switched places, but I must say I was weary of Rex's little dump.

The phone rang. It was Rex.

"I rented my waiter uniform," he said.

"Wonderful . . . you're a dear."

"I'm practicing with your serving tray. Come over for early dinner, I'll wait on you."

"Spare me."

"Something happened to Gershwin—"

"Oh no . . . I'm so sorry—"

"He stopped singing and started talking."

"Come on—"

"You know how I turn on his tape recorder when I go out to maybe pick up some of his singing while I'm not there?"

"Well?"

"I just played the new tape and right in the middle of his singing this guy's voice interrupts him."

"Oh my God—"

"Just when Gershwin's hitting some neat high notes, like two octaves above high C—"

"Pinkus maybe?" I said, not caring about the canary's octaves.

"Could be."

"What day did you record?"

"Night, you mean. Don't remember exactly. Not long after we switched apartments."

"Had to be after the rock."

"Right."

"What'd the guy say, for Godsakes?"

"Couldn't understand it."

"Not even a word or two?"

"Sounds like he was on the phone. Like calling somebody."

"That's what phones are for."

"Don't be a wiseass."

"Sorry, dear. I'm nervous."

"Your phone's too far from Gershwin's recorder to pick up what he said. It was like a far away echo."

"You can't understand any of it?"

" 'Nottingham', I think he said . . . and 'bitch.' "

"Be right over."

"I'll put on my waiter outfit."

As I was rushing out of Rex's, his phone rang and it was a woman's voice. A young woman's voice.

"Please tell him Plucky Duncan called," she said.

"Any message?"

"No, just tell him Plucky called."

Plucky, such a cutie-pie name.

I steamed out the door.

As he let me in my apartment, Rex smiled and leaned down to kiss me. I ducked away.

"What's wrong?"

"Who'd you think I was, Plucky?"

"Whatta you talking about?" he said.

"Plucky Duncan—"

"You saw her?"

"No, sex maniac, she called you."

"Good, I was expecting to hear—"

I stomped across the room like a hurt child.

"Probably about tomorrow night's job. Hope she can make it."

I suddenly got it. My nasty little mind should have been spanked.

"Plucky's my bass player."

"Sorry I'm such an ass, dear, but I love you."

"Stop worrying. She's happily married to a flute player in the Symphony. Pluck's my right hand man . . . woman . . . helps me manage the band. Keeps the girls in line—"

"Women," I said.

"They're pretty young for women."

I gave up.

"The tape. Let's hear the tape."

He pressed the button and penetrating canary chirps came out of the tiny speaker. Hearing it, Gershwin started singing live with his tape. Chalk on a blackboard.

Rex smiled and said, "Listen to that vibrato—"

"Please, Rex, get to the man's voice."

Fast forward and on came a distant, hollow-sounding string of words from a man with a middle range voice. I couldn't understand any of it.

We played it over and over, backwards and forwards. Loud and soft. Impossible to tell who it was and what he said.

"Can you slow it down?" I said.

Rex rewound and played it at low speed.

"You were right, dear. I heard my name . . . and 'bitch'."

"Lamar, maybe?" Rex said. "Gays say 'bitch' a lot. Maybe H-M sent him."

We listened again.

One of the trillion little cells in my brain was trying to tell me who it was, but wasn't getting through.

$\triangledown$

D Day Minus 1

I'D MELTED AWAY TO a size 8 and the old black gown hung on me like a bag. So I took in the frayed seams again to have it ready for the Opera Ball.

Sweet Rex had given me a zirconium necklace for the Ball. He said it would look like diamonds for at least a year, particularly at night, and when he'd paid up his alimony I'd have real diamonds.

At the *Our Crowd* office, Pammie Quackenbush was goosebumps over the upcoming Opera Ball, flittering around like a moth attacking a lightbulb, driving everyone nuts.

For a fifty year old living cadaver, Pammie was rather attractive. But when she spoke her nose flickered like an Easter bunny's, negating her regal charm. You felt like offering her a carrot to munch on.

"This will be our finest ow-ah, Patty deah—"

It sure will, I thought. If she only knew.

"Our biggest and best issue ev-ah." Flicker, flicker.

"We'll knock 'em dead, Pammie," I said. "Make H-M's *Journal* coverage look like a high school paper."

"The old bitch deserves it," she said. "And I've good news for you, deah. I'm giving you an extra photographer to help you and Eddie."

Dear God, I thought. I didn't need someone in my way.

"That's so thoughtful, Pammie, but Eddie's as good as two photographers."

"But I want scads of photos, Patty deah. Our fashion writer Sandy Blackbush has volunteered. She takes divine pictures."

Sandy, young daughter of socialites Keeky and Bucky Blackbush, would use a Polaroid she got for Christmas last year.

"Thank you Pammie." What else could I say?

I planned to keep Sandy away from my stakeout spot. Send her off to get shots of people dancing.

Meanwhile the voice on the canary tape was driving me crazy. It had to be the murderer. Why else would he be in my apartment? Nothing had been stolen. And what a nerve, using my phone. Who was he calling? Rex could be right; gay men do say "bitch" a lot, but it didn't sound like Lamar's squeaky voice. I wondered if he'd sent one of his space cadets.

I thought again about seeing the police, but if I took them a tape of a canary they'd put me in a cage too. I decided to screw the police. I was now an investigative reporter/detective ready to catch the "perp" myself.

Rex wanted to have the tape analyzed. His friend Steve at Coast Sound Studio had recording equipment that could detect the sound of peach fuzz falling on cotton puffs. Rex said Steve was a master and could maybe help me recognize the voice.

Early that evening Rex and I discussed in detail how we'd handle things if we caught the murderer in action.

To have proof on videotape, Eddie would shoot with his 8MM vidcam with a zoom lens. Earlier in the evening we'd take stills of the guests at Mimmsy's table to establish their identity and exactly where they sat.

"There'll be no cops around," Rex said.

"I know, and that's good. They won't get credit for the collar."

"You sure know cop language, but how do we hold onto the son of a bitch?"

"Or her?" I said.

"Could be."

"You're strong, dear, you can hold on 'til we get help."

"Thanks a lot. Maybe there'll be a house detective."

"Not in the Opera House."

"Security guards?"

"At the doors, but awfully far from our stakeout."

"Stakeout . . . you're hot stuff."

"You think I'm just a dumb society columnist?"

"So what do we do?" Rex said.

"Borrow some handcuffs."

He smiled. "We're not allowed to make an arrest, sweetheart. That's against the law."

"So forget the handcuffs. The other waiters'll help you. They'll think you're in their union. And I'll send for a security guard."

"Most security guards are so old, they can hardly stand up."

"You'll handle it, dear. I have faith in you."

"What'll I tell Pronto Uniform Rental when I return my waiter's outfit all wrecked?"

"I've got another idea," I said.

"What?"

"I'll have Myra Bamburger standing by as a reporter witness."

"Bad idea."

"Why?" I said.

"You can't trust anchor women."

"Why?"

"They can't stop blabbing. She'll blow the whole trap if you tell her."

"You're right . . . and she couldn't see that far with her teleprompter syndrome."

"What's that?"

"A long story. Tell you later."

Rex suddenly snapped up in his chair. "What about Max Pinkus?"

"Are you kidding?" I said.

"If he's there when you catch the murderer, he'll really put you on the map."

"I can't stand that creep."

"You can make a million dollar deal with him."

"I'll think about it."

Maybe not a bad idea. I loved Rex's tricky little mind. Smart, too, but you'd never know it by the way he acted.

Rex's friend Steve was in Los Angeles recording music tracks for television commercials. Rex called Steve who told him to drop off the canary tape at coast Sound Studio so he could get at it when he returned.

▽

Play Ball

Every year the opera Ball draws all the city's well born, ordinary rich, and every climber in the area. Every year it's held at our beautiful Opera House, where dining tables are jammed into the huge cathedral-like lobby area. The dancing takes place on the opera stage, and from the pit below the stage the orchestra plays dance music, also piped into the lobby where the guests dine. In the past few years tickets had soared to $1,000 per person or $10,000 for a table of ten, with no discount. They always let me in free.

Eddie and I got there early to photograph arriving couples walking up the white marble stairs, Academy Award style. I expected a frantic night, with my *Our Crowd* duties plus looking for the murderer.

Limousines came in droves to let off guests. Men were in white tie and women in fabulous gowns costing enough to bail out the farm belt. I saw one woman wearing Lamar's crazy "Galactic Woman: 3000"—it was Sophie Jacobs. But no husband Morris. Word was he stopped his hypertension pills because they made him impotent. Morris was now in an urn at the Neptune Society.

The marble walls inside the lobby amplified the crowd noise, until it sounded like a gym with the home team winning. A mix of great perfumes and cigarette smoke permeated the air. (The oldies were still smoking like crazy.) I was off the evil weed, almost.

The biggies had preferred tables, their seating arrangements the same as at the other balls. Place cards were all in place. Mrs. Huntting-Margate, who'd run the affair forever, needed help and had chosen Mimmsy Rittenhouse as her co-chairwoman. My list showed H-M's and Mimmsy's table had Lamar, Prudence and Booly, Meggie and Reggie von Keltz, opera director Dolph Nurenburg with bulging wife Freda, and, of course, Rod Rittenhouse.

During the regular opera season, the mezzanine bar was always a madhouse with people panicking for fixes before curtain time. At the Ball the bar situation was worse. Extra bars had been set up and everyone was jammed together with barely room to stand.

Squeezing into the bar was Reggie von Keltz, the effeminate Nazi, and his haughty wife Meggie who was Reggie's dental hygienist before they were married. I caught Shotsie Fenner nuzzling up to Doctor Booly and figured she'd get him in the sack yet. Shotsie's date was *not* Dudley Crenshaw; she was with Huntley Haverstock, which got me thinking.

I got a little teary when I saw sweet Peter Knapp rushing over to see me.

"I miss you, Patty."

"Even my boring column?"

He smiled. "The new one's worse than yours, Patty. Young Mittsy Stranglesmith from Want Ads writes it."

"Doesn't her father collect golf balls?"

"That's the one. Her mother, Pussy, is a friend of H-M's."

"You poor thing," I said, and kissed him on the cheek.

Then I saw adorable little Pele de Sousa, wearing a silver lame turtle neck under his tail coat. Exhausted, no doubt, after coifing so many ladies for the event, but Pele wouldn't miss the social event of the year.

The clock said 7:50. Dinner was at 8 but it never started on time.

Eddie and I were snapping shots of chatting drinkholders. The *Journal* ran many such pictures on its social pages, but *Our Crowd* held the world's record for shots of chatting drinkholders. I kept scribbling names in my notebook like crazy as Eddie's camera flashed every second.

My big night and I was a wreck. Rex's friend Steve hadn't made it back from L.A. in time to analyze the canary tape so we had no clues from that.

8:00. The bars lights dimmed and the crowd drifted like a human waterfall down to their dinner tables in the lobby.

Wine corks began popping at the tables and the overworked waiters were running around the tables scaling plates of smoked salmon at us like they were dealing black jack.

Our elegant opera lobby sounded like a jetport the day before Christmas.

Before Eddie and I took our seats we got a few more shots of people who wouldn't be rubber stamped, plus the mandatory photo of director Nurenburg.

We could hear Hiro Hakahudo tuning up his orchestra in the pit. Hiro had come a long way from his childhood in Tulare County's World War II detention camp. The program said we'd hear a few excerpts from *Barber of Chernobyl* and *Suicide Suite* during dinner, in honor of Phil Toakhime (and his million dollar opera contribution). Joy to the World, I thought. Excerpts only.

I figured if Mimmsy were to get poisoned, it would be after dinner during champagne and dancing; that had been the pattern. I'd asked Rex to get there earlier though. I'd already given him a plan of table locations and seating arrangements for his surveillance assignment.

At 8:35 I saw him coming toward me. He looked cute in his maroon tails and little yellow towel over his arm. A handsome waiter, except he could barely carry a plate from his kitchen table to his sink. He was wearing sunglasses, and I hoped he'd be able to see what was going on.

Eddie and I sat two tables from Mimmsy's. While Eddie started getting his video camera ready for Rex's signals, I noticed Shotsie and Huntley were sitting at the table between us.

Toakhime's dreadful compositions plus the gymnasium noise were driving me crazy. I felt indigestion coming on and I hadn't even eaten my appetizer.

No speeches were made at the Opera Ball. Just a good time. The event always raised a bundle, but the Opera Company cried poverty every year. What they did with all the money was beyond me.

Entrees of Filet Mignon and tiny carrots were flipped in front of us like Frisbees by the maroon-tailed black jack dealers. And the cabernet was flowing. A great dinner, but I couldn't taste it, and after dessert I knew I'd be a basket case.

Rex was walking around Mimmsy's table trying to look like a busy waiter. He'd removed his sunglasses so he could see.

9:00. Entrees were almost finished and dessert and coffee were set up on serving tables. Rex was trying to avoid the other waiters, but I saw a sweaty fat one hand him a trayful of dirty dishes that stopped Rex in his tracks. The fat waiter reminded me of Rudolph Huntting-Margate, Junior, which reminded me I'd never before seen Junior at the Opera Ball or any other ball.

9:30. Cherries Jubilee was served with coffee.

9:55. The waiters started putting champagne in the ice buckets by the tables and the serious dancing and partying began. The orchestra was playing "Night and Day" and couples were already dancing on the stage.

I saw Rex finesse his tray of dirty dishes to a young busboy.

Eddie, with his loaded video camera, was staring at Rex, waiting for a signal. Rex's eyes kept scanning the table and so did mine.

By now most couples had gone into the theater to dance on the stage. The orchestra segued into "I Get a Kick Out of You." Fluted crystal glasses were on the tables waiting for the champagne.

Booly and Mimmsy had left the table to dance. So had Reggie von Keltz and Freda Nurenberg. Meggie von Keltz, Rod Rittenhouse, Lamar, Prudence and Dolph Nurenberg were still at their table chatting. Their waiter hadn't yet opened the Dom Perignon (most of the nouveaux had ordered Kristal). I saw H-M motor off to circulate in her wheelchair, recently equipped with a green oxygen tank—probably for emphysema.

I looked over at Rex to make sure he was checking the empty champagne glasses.

Eddie had taken establishing shots of people at the table and was standing by with his Sony vidcam.

Then suddenly Rex began waving, pointing down at Lamar who'd just put a flower in Meggie's hair. I saw Meggie smile at the romantic gesture and Rex kept pointing and waving like mad as Eddie rolled his vidcam. I left my table and walked over behind Rex who was leaning over Meggie to see if Lamar had dropped anything in her drink. He got too close, bumping her head with his chest, and accidentally knocked the flower out of her hair.

Rex tried to apologize, but Meggie lost her social demeanor and started bitching at him in her Passaic, New Jersey accent telling him to watch his fucking step.

Then Rex went for Lamar, but I stopped him before he could grab the little worm.

Pulling Rex away, I whispered in his ear, "Meggie von Keltz was a dental hygienist."

"Lousy job. I'd rather be a waiter."

"Don't you get it, dear? She's not eligible for murder. Not in our profile. Remember our victim criteria?"

"Just trying to be helpful," Rex said, backing sheepishly away as I returned to my table.

Meanwhile Eddie had turned off his vidcam.

Just as I sat down, Rex began waving his arms again, pointing down at the table. Eddie snapped on his zoom lens, started rolling the tape and I stood up so I could see better, figuring someone was fiddling with a champagne glass. Everyone at the table seemed to be too busy chatting to notice and Meggie was under the table looking for her flower. One waiter was clearing plates off the table and another waiter had just popped open a bottle of their champagne.

Eddie started his vidcam again, but he'd run out of tape. Great timing. He grabbed for a new cassette, taking too damned long to find it. We had to get that shot.

Rex was pointing to . . . My God, I thought, was it Prudence? Rex was miming something that looked like unwrapping a package. And he was mouthing something . . . like he was "booing" at a football game.

Eddie found his new cassette, took forever to peel off the wrapper, frantically reloaded his vidcam and started rolling just as Prudence dropped the stuff into the champagne glass. Yes, it was Prudence Jabbar-Lamumba.

Rex grabbed the glass, waved me over to come get it and then grabbed Prudence who jumped out of her chair and began struggling to get away. One waiter thought Rex was bananas and tried to pull him away from Prudence as I ran over and yelled at the waiter that she was trying to poison someone, showing him the empty champagne glass with the little yellow stick in the bottom of its stem.

"I don't see nothin'," The waiter said.

"It's way down in the bottom. Tough to see."

"So howdyknow it's poison, lady?" he asked.

"Wanna try some?" I said.

After the Ball

THE WAITER BELIEVED ME and helped Rex restrain Prudence.

Eddie'd videotaped everything, including Prudence caught in the act and a closeup of me showing the poison stick in the bottom of the glass. The glass had been at Booly's place setting. It wasn't Mimmsy this time. The victim was to be Booly.

There wasn't much confusion, because most everyone was dancing, including Booly and Mimmsy. The few people left at surrounding tables didn't seem that concerned—probably thought Prudence was drunk.

Rod Rittenhouse ran off to find Mimmsy. Lamar left in a snit, and Meggie von Keltz, smashed by then and wanting to dance, was tugging at old Dolph Nurenberg, glassy-eyed and oblivious to what was happening.

Another waiter returned with two security guards—a decrepit old man, probably earning a few extra bucks, and a young black guy who looked like he could handle the situation.

I wrapped the poisoned glass in a napkin and put it in my shoulder bag. Then I followed Rex and the young security guard, dragging Prudence—fighting like a mad woman, yelling she'd "get the son-of-a-bitch" and calling everyone "rotten snobs"—outside to the front steps of the opera house where we hailed a police car parked nearby. The old security guard was out of it, still trying to negotiate the long marble stairway.

Two cop cars with screaming sirens took us to the Bryant Street station. Rex, Eddie and I in one car—the other car, with a wire cage between the back and front seats, carried Prudence, whose diamond tiarra was more than askew by then.

They booked Prudence Jabbar-Lamumba on suspicion of something-or-other and took her to a cell. Without positive proof that the stuff was poison, they couldn't charge her with attempted murder. A big police sergeant asked Eddie to empty his cameras, and I gave the poison glass to a cop who took it and dashed out of the room—to their lab for analysis I assumed.

Crime reporters had already questioned homicide before we got there. When the reporters saw us they asked a few questions and Rex told me to establish that I was the one, and not the cops, who planned and caught the criminal, which I did but they didn't seem to care that much.

Then a cop took us into homicide for Q and A and to fill out forms . . . and there he was—Lieutenant Kilarney with a smug smile on his fat face. I gave Kilarney my "I told you so" look, and he said, "Nice of you to help us with this one Miz Nottingham."

"Help you? I caught her myself, Lieutenant Kilarney," I shouted. "With no help from you people."

"Don't get your blood pressure up, Miz Nottingham," he said and walked out of the room.

About six cops led Rex, Eddie and me out of the station. Television crews were outside the building anxiously waiting to get inside. I smiled for the cameras like an actress on opening night, hoping they'd take our pictures, but the police rushed us through the crowd into a cab.

After letting Eddie off at his flat on Pine Street, we went

to my apartment which slobbo and his noisy canary were still occupying. It was late—2 A.M.

In bed, too hyped-up and euphoric to sleep, we talked about our victory—surprised and shocked that Prudence was the murderer and that she'd intended to poison her husband and not Mimmsy, whom we'd predicted as the target.

"Bertrand Russell was right," Rex said.

"About what?"

"One never knows what lurks in the heart of woman."

"Goodnight."

Just before we drifted off, Rex asked, "What the hell was her motive?"

"God knows, but homicide will grill it out of her. We'll know tomorrow."

"G'night famous investigative journalist celebrity of San Francisco."

Just a Woman and a
Waiter

ON THE MORNING NEWS, Myra Bamburger was interviewing Lieutenant Kilarney, who said, "We're grateful for the cooperation we got from those people at the Opera affair, Myra. If more citizens would help us policemen a little more there'd be less crime and we could balance the scales of justi—"

I had to say it: "Shit. Shit. Shit," I yelled. "Kilarney's a dirty lying bastard."

Rex woke up and said, "That's no way for a society writer to talk."

I pointed him to the television set.

". . . Yes, Myra," Kilarney was saying, "Arresting Denton and Steinbrenner was purely subterfuge to make the real perp think the police had closed the case."

"What crap," I said.

"He's taking credit, for chrissake," Rex said.

". . . but," said Myra. "You've put the doctors through hell, Lieutenant."

"They'll get over it, Myra," Kilarney said, smiling.

That's what you think you rotten son of a bitch, I said under my breath.

Myra continued. "If I were Doctor Denton or Doctor

159

Steinbrenner, I'd be more than upset, Lieutenant—"

"The department'll present them our citizens award for meritorious service. Maybe give one to that little woman at the dance who helped us. Good publicity for them."

Dirty bastard wouldn't even mention my name. I couldn't stand it any longer and shut the television off. My fame and fortune had dissolved to nothing.

The *Journal* headlined the arrest of the "Balls of Death" killer, showing Kilarney with his hands in the air like Richard Nixon. Inside was a picture of cops and reporters with Rex and me in back of them so you couldn't recognize us. Buried in the article they mentioned that a woman and a waiter at the party had helped the police.

"Helped them? May Kilarney rot in hell," I shouted.

Reading on, the paper said Prudence would be arraigned next week. Rex saw I was destroyed and put his arms around me as I turned on *Mr. Coffee*.

"Things could be worse Patty—"

"No they couldn't. Life is unfair." I began to cry.

"You still have the thing in the lemon sorbet."

"Makes no difference," I sobbed. "The cops have the glass with the stuff at the police station. And Eddie's tapes."

"You can tell them about your analysis—"

"City Hall's in bed with Kilarney, Rex. They have to be. Nobody'll listen to some stupid society writer from *Our Crowd* for godsakes."

"You saved Booly's life, Patty. You should be proud."

"And everyone thought Prudence adored him," I sobbed.

"Maybe he threatened to add her to his shrunken head collection."

I couldn't help but smile.

"Wonder what her motive was," Rex said, wiping the tears from my cheek.

"We'll find out at the trial. They should subpoena us," I said, calming down.

"I'll take you to a nice lunch today. We'll forget about the damned thing."

"We just had breakfast."

"With white tablecloths and a full bar." Rex said. "We'll make it brunch."

"Good. I need a drink."

$\triangledown$

Why Did She?

I SAT IN THE courtroom during the entire trial. They called me to the stand but asked me only a few questions. I tried to explain to the judge and D.A. that the police had nothing to do with catching Prudence and that I'd done all the work, but they sloughed me off as though I were crazy.

They called Rex up for a few questions and he tried to give me credit, but they ignored him too.

If I'd had a gun I would have used it on Kilarney, the way he lied on the witness stand, taking all the credit for his "investigative strategy" to catch the murderer. He'd known all along it was poison, he said. But he never explained what kind it was. Just poison. Period. No explanation of the autopsies. Nothing. A shallow case with many loose ends, but City Hall wanted a conviction without any more expense.

On the stand, Prudence—looking like she'd been on a week's drunk—admitted she'd poisoned Binky, Neenie and Buffy, but refused to tell what the poison was or where she got it.

"You're so goddamned smart. Find out for yourselves," she said pulling at her tangled red hair and sticking out her tongue.

"Order," said Judge Barrola, tapping his gavel.

"Shove your little hammer," Prudence shouted.

"You're in contempt," Barrola said, his cheek veins glowing red.

"So send me to jail, fatso," she screamed, jumping up from the witness chair.

A strapping, uniformed woman rushed over and grabbed Prudence, who began flailing her arms as she was dragged out of the courtroom yelling, "Those snot bitches cut me out of their precious Social Register, and that wasn't enough . . ."

Her voice trailed off and we couldn't hear the rest of what she said.

I remembered when Prudence was removed from the Register, after she married Boolibar. (We society journalists automatically receive such world-shaking news.) But why commit murder over such a petty thing?

After a ten minute recess the trial resumed, and defense attorney Bellevue Paunche—whose objective was to save Prudence from San Quentin's cyanide pellet so he could milk her for mistrial and appeal fees the rest of her life—called up a surprise witness: Pele de Sousa, hairdresser to society's first team.

Adorable little Pele featured a modified Mohawk with long hair in back flowing over his stylishly oversized silvery, raw silk suit, big enough for Bubba Paris of the 49ers. I figured Pele had been subpoenaed for some hot news from his "gossip central" salon on Maiden Lane. Now I wished I'd thought of interviewing him during my investigation.

". . . yes, sir," Pele said. "Binky, Neenie and many of my lovely ladies were seeing Doctor Boolibar for his youth medicine—"

"Did they go to the doctor for more than his medicine, Mr. de Sousa?" asked Paunche . . .

In the end Prudence confirmed that her hairdresser Pele's gossip was true. Binky, Neenie, Buffy and others had been sneaking to her beloved husband Booly to sip from his "fountain of sexual youth," and some had stayed for phase two with stud Booly to satisfy the desires brought on by his concoction. Lifts and tucks from Denton weren't enough. They wanted to *feel* young, too.

Too much a lady to do such a thing, Mimmsy Rittenhouse hadn't been mentioned during gossip at Pele's network. All along I'd thought she missed being poisoned because she'd given up alcohol and didn't drink champagne.

Prudence had adored Booly who'd given her a new and wonderful life, and she went crazy when she discovered her best friends and husband had disgraced and betrayed her.

Rex had moved back to his own apartment, but was at my place more than his. Sitting on my couch in our terry robes, we talked about the case.

"Drumming her out of the bluebook for marrying Booly gave her a running start, but what pushed her over the edge was her lady friends screwing around with her new husband."

"Why so excited about the bluebook?" Rex asked.

"Prudence was incensed that they'd broken a limb in her Lansdale-Chase family tree tracing back to the Earl of Schrewsbury."

"Never heard of him."

"I feel kind of sorry for Prudence."

"Booly didn't say a word in court."

"He didn't want to testify, and didn't have to."

"Booly's a nice guy, but a bit horny."

"Better watch yourself."

"Prudence was getting away with murder, Patty. If it wasn't for you—"

"You inspired me, dear."

I thought back to the Symphony dance . . . if Mimmsy hadn't given up alcohol she'd have drunk the champagne and stiffened up like the others, and I'd never have found the pale yellow stick in her unfilled glass that night. Prudence thought she had put it in Booly's glass. He sat next to Mimmsy that night.

"That's some crazy poison whatever it is," Rex said. "Where the hell did she get it?"

"She refused to tell and City Hall doesn't care. They've got their conviction. I'm just a nobody and Kilarney's a hero. Life is unfair."

"So's death," Rex said.

"I'll expose that bastard Kilarney if it kills me."

"That's the spirit . . . So what about Denton and Steinbrenner?"

"They sprung the poor guys from jail."

"They'll sue the city for a fortune."

"I hope so, and they'll have the enormous resources of the Cosmetic and Plastic Surgeons Association to help them."

"Here's to it," Rex said, kissing my cheek.

$\triangledown$

Pru Perfect Poison

THE RELENTLESS PRESS JARRED Mayor Skiathos from his deep sleep, forcing him to do a number on City Hall and the police department fast. First to go were Lieutenant Kilarney, Judge Barrola and D.A. Stavros Feta.

New D.A. Clarence Banks dug into the investigation of the police's handling of the case with vigor, reviewing an Opera Ball videotape with me and analyzing the poison stick I'd finally removed from my lemon sorbet. Kilarney had disposed of the poisoned champagne glass and videotape, but Eddie hadn't given them the cassette from his carrying case which contained enough evidence to corroborate that my team had made the collar.

Prudence eventually told police she'd obtained the poison from her husband's lab without Booly's knowledge. At my suggestion Banks hired Marlowe Tweed and Herman Kleindienst of Jack London Chemists to investigate Booly's lab to determine what the stuff was.

"Tell me about the wild poison," said Rex.
"It was from Booly's lab."
"Thought he was trying to make people live longer—"
"What made the ladies puff and stiff, even before rigor mortis could set in, was an overdose of snake venom mixed

166

with testosterone and other gross things from testicles of bulls from Booly's ranch in Chad."

"I'll have to get some of that—"

"You don't need it yet."

I explained how testosterone had something to do with causing tumescence.

"So the ladies died of hard ons?"

"No dear, they stiffened when their central nervous system was hit with the mamba venom—"

"Sounds like a rock group."

"Please . . . In his experiments, Booly mixed only a very weak, diluted venom solution with the stuff from the Chad bull balls. The combination over activated the adrenal glands in his lab animals, giving the males enormous energy to work off their abnormal tumescence. And the females became insatiable."

"I remember you told me how they humped themselves silly."

"Knowing where Booly stored everything," I said. "Prudence sneaked some undiluted, straight snake venom and mixed it with the waxy testosterone so it could be handled and shaped to fit in the bottom of the champagne glasses."

"Booly damn near got killed with his own stuff and knew nothing about it?"

"Not a thing."

"Hell of a life extension program."

"He thinks he's found it."

"Chad's Ponce de Leon."

Rex asked how come the autopsies showed nothing unusual.

"First of all," I said. "The autopsies were perfunctorily performed."

"Say that three times fast."

"You're really irritating today," I said, unable to keep from smiling.

"Sorry. Just happy for you, that's all," he said, kissing my cheek and putting his hand inside my terry robe.

"Prudence knew Booly'd killed some lab animals while experimenting with various combinations of his venom, bull stuff and whatever. And he'd told her how surprised he was that hardly any evidence of poison showed up in autopsies he'd performed on the dead hamsters."

"She was a shrewd broad," Rex said, squeezing my thigh.

"I still think schmucko Kilarney avoided pressing the autopsies to skip a long investigation. Used poor Denton and Steinbrenner as scapegoats."

"Kilarney's ass is history."

"I love it."

Love that Canary

GETTING DRESSED THE NEXT morning Rex said, "And we thought it could've been that Lamar creep dropping stuff in their champagne while he was fooling around with the flowers."

"Just being nice to the ladies."

"Trying to sell some dresses, you mean."

The phone rang. It was Steve, the recording genius.

"It's too late for our murder mystery, Steve, but I'd like to see you anyway."

Rex hung up and told me Steve had isolated the voice.

"Probably Pinkus or one of his sleazeballs. Makes no difference now."

"Let's go anyway. You'll enjoy Steve, and I want to talk to him about recording my band."

Sitting at a console with thousands of buttons and things that slid up and down, Steve waved us into his glassed-in studio. He was recording the last line of a radio commercial.

"Once more, Mel. Hit every word this time."

Behind a glass wall in a tiny padded room, Mel boomed into the microphone: "AND EVEN IF YOU'RE ON DEATH ROW, YOU'LL GET CREDIT AT DAVID'S DIA-MOND EMPORIUM."

"Only terrific, Mel," Steve shouted, smiling through his red handlebar mustache. "It's a wrap."

Steve stood up and hugged Rex. "Been too long, buddy."
"I know, Stevo." Rex towered over Steve's wiry little body.
Rex introduced me and Steve said, "You in his sexy new band?"
"You flatter me," I said, loving Steve already.
"Can you record them?" Rex said.
"Can't wait to see your girls."
"They play music too, Stevo."
They arranged a recording date and Steve said, "Want to hear that voice on your canary tape?"
We said we'd love to, and Steve rigged up a large spool of wide tape and gave me big earphones to put on.
He fiddled with his switches and buttons, then fast forwarded the canary part until he got to the voice which he'd isolated by removing all the background and echo sounds.
I heard a man's voice but didn't recognize it. Too soft so I asked Steve to make it louder which he did by pushing more buttons.
Suddenly I got it. "It's *him*," I shouted.
"Who?" Rex said.
"That bastard Kilarney."
"You sure?"
Steve rewound and played the tape again . . . No doubt about it. It was Kilarney in *my* apartment on *my* phone calling someone.
I took off my earphones and thanked Steve. "You're a genius."
My life's renewed, I thought.
"How can I ever repay you?" I said.
"A pleasure, Ma'am," he smiled. "Just keep takin' good care of my buddy Rex here."
Rex wanted to pay Steve, but he wouldn't take a cent. He made two cassettes for us and said he'd keep the master in his files.
At the door Steve hugged us goodbye and said, "Love to meet your canary some day. He blows good."

⊽

Myra's Exclusive

I CALLED MYRA BAMBURGER who would sell her mother for a good story and told her I had information related to her "Balls of Death" story that could destroy City Hall and the Homicide department.

"That's old news, Miss Nottingham," she said in her snotty way.

"I've got proof Lieutenant Kilarney unlawfully broke into my apartment and threatened me with death if I didn't stop my investigation of Binky, Neenie and Buffy."

"I want an exclusive then."

I knew Myra still had a low opinion of Kilarney and the birds at City Hall.

"You've got it."

"Come to my office."

I brought the badly typewritten note, the rock message and Gershwin's tape that Steve had processed.

"These could have been written by anyone," Myra said, shuffling the notes in her newscaster hands.

"But this tape corroborates it was Kilarney."

She put the tape in her portable recorder, turned it on and the canary started blasting.

"I haven't time for practical jokes," she said.

As she reached to turn it off, the man's voice came on:

171

"I'm at . . . bitch . . . Nottingham's . . . place . . . no . . . can't find a th—"

"That *is* Kilarney," she said, smiling.

"I told you—"

"I'll interview you this afternoon for tonight's news, Patty."

At 6 o'clock that evening Rex and I watched Myra Bamburger report what she called her "post script" to "Balls of Death". She read the notes, played the tape and showed old interview tapes of Kilarney condemning Denton and Steinbrenner. Myra destroyed Kilarney, proving him the sneaky ass he was. Then she played my taped interview and I didn't look too bad except the closeups made me seem very fortyish: ". . . Yes, Myra, I knew all along the doctors were innocent . . . ."

I told Myra about finding and analyzing the poison and how I'd spent weeks investigating, and how despicable I thought Kilarney and City Hall were to take the credit for my collar. My interview lasted four full minutes.

Kilarney had tried to frighten me. Keep me from continuing my investigation. He thought I knew something and feared I'd embarrass his Homicide department. He'd be more than embarrassed now. I couldn't wait 'til they nailed the bastard and whoever was in on it with him.

Rex grabbed me and said, "Now they know Patty Nottingham's the real hero."

"Heroine," I said, and kissed him.

Queen of the Hilton

MY PHONE RANG LIKE crazy. Congratulations from friends, the social set, the climbers. Requests for media interviews. Literary agents. Hollywood agents. Stock brokers. Pinkus. On and on. H-M's secretary called and asked me to come in, and I told her I was too busy.

Even Peter called to wish me well. "Too bad the old bat wasn't around to take a sip," he said.

I laughed. "Maybe Junior will take care of her."

Newspapers announced my story in banner headlines. Every television channel reported how "Patty Nottingham had trapped Prudence Landsdale-Chase Jabbar-Lamumba, and not the police." Columnists and television newscasters crucified Kilarney for his behavior.

Until Pammie Quackenbush found my replacement, I was helping her with *Our Crowd* and her staff was treating me like royalty.

Meanwhile offers kept pouring in for books, magazine articles, television mini-series and other things. Rex insisted I get an agent.

One of the pink message slips on my desk the day after the Bamburger interview said to call a Ransom Blocker of ASCAP, collect.

"Blocker here. Thank you for returning my call, Miss Nottingham.

"You've probably called the wrong number, sir. I'm not in music."

"I don't understand, Miss Nottingh—"

"Aren't you the society of music composers and publishers?"

I heard him chuckle. "Oh no," he said. "American Society of Cosmetic and Plastic Surgeons. I'm Doctor Ransom Blocker, president."

"So sorry, Doctor—"

"Do you realize what you've done for our profession, Miss Nottingham?"

Good. He was calling about my vindicating Denton and Steinbrenner.

"It was nothing," I said. "I knew the doctors were innocent."

"We want to honor you at our convention."

I told him I'd love it. He said the convention was at the New York Hilton starting the following Wednesday and that he'd send me plane tickets.

Before he hung up, he said, We've got a little surprise for you Wednesday night, Miss Nottingham."

"I can't wait . . . and call me Patty."

"And you can call me Ransom."

Walking off the 747 into the passenger area I saw a chauffeur holding up a little white cardboard sign with my name on it. I waved to him, he greeted me on behalf of ASCAPS, led me to a white stretch limousine and told me my baggage would be delivered to the hotel.

The V.I.P. treatment. I loved it.

In minutes we were inching our way into New York City. Denton and Steinbrenner were in the Hilton lobby and went bananas when they saw me—hugged and kissed me and thanked me for saving their lives.

That night the convention kicked off in the grand ballroom with yours truly on the podium—wondering about the "little surprise"—in my new size 8 red ball gown and zirconium necklace that still looked like diamonds.

With me on the podium were Doctors Ransom Blocker, Clyde Steinbrenner, Clinton Denton and other skin stretchers whose names I forgot.

Blocker, a boring, forgettable looking man, gave the keynote address, boasting about their profession's "contribution to making the world brighter for those who'd been ravaged by Father Time and puffed up by fatty calories."

I could barely keep from laughing.

He droned on about new cosmetic surgery techniques and told us that they'd demonstrate these breakthrough methods during the convention.

That afternoon I'd met a lot of the doctor's wives and couldn't tell one from the other. Each of them with their perky little noses and wide eyes, looked the same age. I have this vision that one day all older women will look alike.

Blocker finished his speech and then presented the annual Golden Scalpel award to Dr. Max Wu Wang who'd perfected a technique for modifying eyelids that transformed Asians into Caucasians (or vice versa) in less time than it takes to get your ears pierced.

Then, all smiles, Blocker turned to me. "And now . . . a few words about a courageous young woman, our beautiful guest of honor, Patty Nottingham . . ."

Beautiful and young—nice compliment in this crowd.

". . . without her our profession would be shut down . . . We were already out of business in San Francisco after the cruel arrests of Clyde and Clinton . . . Patty believed in us, and we owe her a great deal for risking her life . . ."

Maybe some money?

". . . we've not only voted Patty ASCAPS Woman of the Year . . . We've also established a trust . . ."

Now you're talking, Ransom.

". . . providing a lifetime income . . . ."

Thank you God.

Blocker motioned for me to stand next to him as he picked up the ASCAPS plaque and an envelope.

Probably a gift certificate for cosmetic surgery of my choice.

". . . This envelope contains your ASCAPS award—a certified check for $150,000—really a reward for your bravery and for giving our profession the lift it needed—please excuse the pun . . . ."

Thank you again God . . . and Rex, Eddie, Prudence Jabbar-Lamumba and Booly's lovely snakes, monkeys and bull balls.

Everyone cheered for an embarrassing length of time. You'd think I'd discovered a cure for Cancer. But I suppose these dudes considered it better than that.

Standing at the microphone, my mouth suddenly stuck together like it had the day Mrs. Huntting-Margate called me to her office. After a sip of water I thanked them, said a few words and ended with something dumb like, "keep your chins up," which I shouldn't have said but it got a big laugh.

When I left the podium, the doctors mobbed me, and I loved every minute of it.

The orchestra began playing, and it sounded too familiar. Could it be? I looked across the room and my God it was Rex with his twelve sexy musicians. The doctors had flown them here just for me. Rex waved and rushed through the crowd to see him. He started playing "That Face" a wonderful song Fred Astaire used to sing, but I don't think the crowd got it.

Anyway, it was a fabulous evening. And to top it off, Rex and I spent the night in the Presidential Suite, that Blocker had booked for us.

Next morning in the lobby, just before I left, Steinbrenner and Denton came up to say goodbye.

"Bye Patty dear," said Denton. Then softly in my ear he said, "And if ever you need a little tuck, come see me. No charge."

"Or a little suck," whispered Steinbrenner.

$\triangledown$

Loose Ends

So WHERE ARE THE rest of them and what are they doing?

PETER KNAPP. My former editor is still at the *Journal* supervising young Mittsy Stranglesmith's society column called "Mittsy's Bits."

MRS. HUNTTING-MARGATE. Lighting a Camel one day with a kitchen match the oxygen bottle on her wheel chair exploded, carbonizing every hair on her head and triggering a severe hearing loss. But she's learned to live with her two 1,000 watt hearing aids hidden by her auburn wig, and Peter's using a klaxon horn to communicate until she can read lips.

My suspicions about H-M were wrong. All along she'd simply wanted to keep me from inflating the scandal of her social set. She's still an old crab though and I'm glad to be free of her.

RUDOLPH HUNTTING-MARGATE, JR. Peter told me Junior bought his mother a new and much larger oxygen bottle.

PRUDENCE, aka #689352. Bellevue Paunche managed to get Prudence three and a half life sentences—the half for attempting to knock off Booly. Paunche is conservator of her blind trust and agent for a book she's writing.

DR. BOOLIBAR JABBAR-LAMUMBA. Booly's still the stud of the social set, seen a lot with young Sandy Blackbush whom he met at the Opera Ball while she was taking *Our Crowd* pictures with her Polaroid. His life extension grant was not renewed, so he donated his humping monkeys to the Quackenbush Monkey pavillion.

Booly never forgets to send a carton of Marlboros every month to Prudence at Camerio Woman's Prison near Fresno where she works in the sheet metal shop stamping out road signs.

LAMAR. Excessive cocaine sniffing burned away the cartilage separating his nostrils and Lamar now has but one gaping hole in his nose, provoking kinky remarks from some nasty people. He's also had Doctor Hubert Short perform a sex change, requiring alterations in his lamé jump suits to accommodate his new little bosom. No one's buying Lamar's idiot gowns, and to make ends meet he occasionally cuts a hundred dozen chenille robes for his former boss in New York, who's still supplying Montgomery Ward.

LIEUTENANT KILARNEY. Kilarney escaped a jail sentence. Instead he was dismissed from the force and stripped of his retirement pay. Now a freelance toll taker, he's often seen working at the entrance to the Oakland Bay Bridge.

DR. CLINTON DENTON. The good doctor's making a fortune lifting and tucking every woman in Mittsy Stranglesmith's column, and he's been nominated for next year's ASCAPS Golden Scalpel award for rehabilitating those unfortunate women on Bombardo's show.

It's still too soon for me to visit him for my payoff but it won't be long.

DR. CLYDE STEINBRENNER. Steinbrenner returned to Salsarita armed with three new pumps and has regained his lucrative practice from the re-fried beans set. Clyde's ex-wife begged to come back but he told her "not over my dead iguana."

MIMMSY AND ROD RITTENHOUSE. Dull stock market conditions have depleted Mimmsy and Rod's portfolio from 80 million to 68 million, but they're hanging in.

SHOTSIE FENNER. Shotsie married Buz Bricker, her twenty-four year old tennis instructor at the Pacific Heights Tennis Club. Buz now manages Shotsie's investments, and is a member, and "A" player for the club.

DUDLEY CRENSHAW, HUNTLEY HAVERSTOCK, AND REDRICK TREXTON. Having all married young Junior Leaguers, Dud, Hunt and Red are enjoying a little extra glow in their golden years.

MARVIN. My pharmacist is still hanging on with white knuckles, paying exorbitant rent to a Hong Kong real estate syndicate who bought his building on Union Street. Marvin's managing to stay afloat with the renewed interest in condom buying plus vigorous sales of lottery tickets which far exceeds the income of his prescription business. He's also improved his same-day film service from four days to three.

MAXIMILLIAN PINKUS. I didn't accept any more of his rag's money, but they wrote my story anyway. Actually it wasn't a bad article and gave me enormous publicity.

SAL MANICOTTI. Sal is funding a feasibility study on filling in the Bay between San Francisco and Oakland with non-biodegradable garbage to create a sixty-two lane road that would eliminate congestion on the Bay Bridge.

His land mine program to discourage graffiti artists is causing controversy, even though Huntley Haverstock has agreed to manufacture the mines at cost in his Road Reminder Corporation factory.

MYRA BAMBURGER. Plagued with "teleprompter fatigue," Myra retired and now lives in the SAG/AFTRA Home for Tired Newscasters. Word is she sits in the ladies' rest room for hours waiting for the john paper to roll out some printed news copy.

MS. FANNIE DOERFLINGER. Fannie's left her post as head of S.O.O.—Save Our Ozone—to form a new group S.O.P.— Save Our Pigeons, but so far has no volunteers.

SOPHIE JACOBS. During Sophie's seventh face lift her chin bone popped through, scaring the hell out of Dr. Denton, who quickly grafted skin from her inner thigh, but even through heavy makeup you notice the doughy little patch.

PELE DE SOUSA. Pele's salon was boycotted by the crowd, forcing him out of business. With the fee Paunche paid him to testify, Pele bought a Super Cuts franchise in Fresno. Once a month he visits Prudence at Camerio Women's Prison to do her hair.

STANLEY HERKIMER. Yes, old Stanley did die of old age, and no amount of fiber could have helped him.

REX AND I. Rex leased a lovely two bedroom apartment in Pacific Heights and I'm happy to say we now live together. Not married yet, but I'm working on it.

His bands are doing beautifully, and so far he's kept his long fingers off the musicians.

My agent and I are busy with a book, a television mini-series to be sponsored by the Cubic Zirconia Cartel, Weight Watchers television commercials, and an endorsement for Kusho walking shoes. Plenty of money, but even when that stops, I can fall back on my ASCAPS trust fund.

If you have enjoyed this book and would like to receive details of other Walker Mystery-Suspense novels, please write for your free catalog:

Walker and Company
720 Fifth Avenue
New York NY 10010